I0619018

EYE OF THE RAVEN

PREQUEL: STORM BLOODLINE SAGA

EMMY R. BENNETT

DREAM SCRIPT MEDIA

Copyright © 2022 Emmy R. Bennett

Published by Dream Script Media LLC

Library of Congress Control Number 1-11409905251

© 2022 Cover by, Lily Dormishev

Edited by Gail Delaney

Edited by Rebecca Jaycox

ISBN: (Ebook) 978-1-950501-08-3

ISBN: (Pbk) 978-1-950501-09-0

DEDICATION

THANK YOU, GRANDMA JUNE, for giving me the encouragement to pursue my dreams. You knew it was possible before I did.

I'm forever grateful. You will be missed.

1

CASTLE SECRETS

WHERE IS IT? IT must be here somewhere. I yank open the first three drawers of the desk and come up empty-handed. I check the next drawer. It's locked.

I'm on borrowed time. Everyone is asleep, and here I am, tiptoeing through the dark castle to the study where my grandfather keeps his documents. If I'm caught, he won't think twice to kill me, even if I'm his blood.

According to Tharin, my beau, these documents are in here somewhere. I need to find them. Tharin said the whole kingdom will die if I don't. It is guaranteed, war will transpire should Grandfather follow through with his orders. At first, I didn't believe a word Tharin said, but then I started adding up certain events that since have occurred. It proves my grandfather, the King of the Underworld, is planning something big.

I take a pin from my hair and work the lock. It takes a bit of effort, but I'm able to pop the latch. I open the drawer only to find it empty.

"No, this can't be," I whisper. A few pens roll as I pull the drawer open more and I feel around for a secret latch, but nothing is there.

Footsteps outside the office door approach, prompting me to close the drawer and quickly hide. Who could be up at this hour? It's two in the morning.

I slip behind the thick drapes next to the window, barely making it in time, and observe the door slowly creaking open. Peeking between the cracks of the velvet curtains, I realize it's Tharin. What's he doing here? I told him I would get the task accomplished. I'm annoyed by his impatience.

He follows the same steps as I did. Even popping the drawer that is empty, only he manages to pull out the documents I didn't see. The same documents he asked me to steal. How is that possible? Why do I get the feeling I'm being played?

As he sifts through the papers, a few pages fall onto the floor, and he proceeds to pick them up.

His back is turned when my grandfather comes strolling in. "How did you get in here?"

I grin because Grandfather loves to sneak up on the unsuspecting. It's one of his many talents.

Tharin stumbles on his words. "I–I was passing the hall, Sire, and noticed your door was ajar."

I think hard. *No, I'm sure I closed it tight. He's lying.*

"And then when I came to inspect your study, this drawer was unlocked." Tharin points where he'd dropped the plans. "I found those on the floor," he lies, again.

Why is Tharin here? I wonder if he's been spying. Is he covering for me so I don't get into trouble, or is he trying to frame me? I'm still hooked on the fact that he pulled the plans out of the same drawer I already checked.

My grandfather narrows his eyes. "You know, Tharin, when I hired you to guard Princess Petra it didn't mean you had the right to come into my study. Calling a guard would have put you in a better favor with me than at present."

"Yes, Sire." Tharin nods.

Grandfather takes in a deep breath. He's always had patience, but that's also what keeps people guessing. His quiet demeanor is what terrifies everyone. We never know what he's thinking. "You may go. I'll deal with you later."

I watch as Tharin dusts something from his hands off onto the scattered pages lying on the floor and in the drawer. What is that? Grandfather didn't see Tharin's silent sleight of hand.

Does Tharin really know I'm here? I watch him exit while Grandfather picks up the papers and tightly stacks them back together. He mumbles something under his breath, but I can't make out what he says, then places them back in the locked drawer, taking the key with him.

That was close. Hurrying from the drapes, I make a second attempt to grab the papers, and this time I'm able to see the documents. There is magic flowing through these walls, and I begin to see precisely what is happening. Not only do I see the plans where I once did not, but a book is also in the same drawer.

What is going on here? I pick it up. It is larger than most volumes with the binding bound in brown leather. The front of the cover reads in gold lettering: *Book of Secrets*.

When I flip open the pages, they're all blank. Why would my grandfather hold such a book as this? If this is important enough to hide, then it's important enough for me to steal, but how am I going to haul this out of here without it being seen? If I'm caught, there will be no way of concealing it.

I pick up grandfather's papers, too, and fold them in half, putting them inside the book. I put everything back as it was and sneak out the door. I must be careful. I wasn't expecting to steal such a large item. Papers can easily be hidden, but this, well, it's rather heavy, too. My arms already ache from holding the book as I pass down the dark hallways back to my living quarters. Avoiding the guards will be tricky. I need to take the back steps the servants use if I want to slip away unnoticed. I skip around the outer edge of the breezeway between my grandfather's living quarters and my parents'. Our palace is grand, almost like it's two separate structures, residing on either side of a sea cliff. The two spaces are separated by a bridge. Below rolls the ocean with rocks that scale the sides. I'll be out in the open when I cross. Thankfully, the dark phase of our moons doesn't show much light during this time, so it makes it easier for me to hide in the shadows.

I come up the back steps to our living quarters and dip inside the corridor. To my right is the long, dark hall that leads back to the sleeping quarters, and to my left is the balcony that overlooks the breezeway from which I came. Mother's alcove sets off to the side where she does her magic rituals.

I'm thankful I looked before passing to my room because I observe two shadows moving, which keep me still against the cold stone wall. Chattering whispers of two familiar voices spark my intrigue.

I shouldn't eavesdrop on such conversations, but when this is my only way back to my room, I have no choice but to listen.

"Are you sure this is going to work?" he asks.

My heart sinks. *Tharin?* I know I shouldn't spy, but curiosity has the better of me.

"It will if you don't screw it up," she says.

5

My stomach churns. I have a hard time swallowing back the bile rising in my throat. Why is my mother speaking to Tharin? *Does she know about us?*

"Just do as I say, and everything will continue as planned," she adds.

"If Vothule finds out—"

"He won't," she interrupts.

"What about Petra?"

"What about her?" I can hear the venom in her tone. "My father favors her because she's the first-born grandchild. If you do exactly as I intend for you to do, it will all fall into place perfectly. Has she fallen in love with you yet?"

Before Tharin can answer, footsteps echo through the dark corridor, prompting them to be quiet.

"Someone's coming. Go. Get out of here before you're seen," she says.

Did my mother cook up a scheme for Tharin to come into my life? I push my back farther against the cold stone wall as the shadow of a man passes in the darkness.

It's my father. "What are you doing out here on the balcony on such a cold night. Darling, you're going to catch a chill."

"Just looking out among the stars, my love." Her malicious tone from earlier vanishes. "No need to check up on me, Octavious. I'm fine." My mother Sarmira is the daughter of none other than the ruler of the underworld, Vothule, my grandfather.

I'm guessing my father has no clue of Mother's deceitfulness.

They step inside from the balcony, and I watch as they move to her small ritual room. Glass shatters, startling me, and it almost foils my eavesdropping. At first, I think it's our cat, knocking off a dish from the alter table butted against a wall, in Mother's alcove, but then my father asks, "Why not use a knife, Sarmira?"

Panic flows through my veins. Oh no, she's starting the ritual now. I didn't think she'd go through with it while guests arrive for the celebration of my birthday, scheduled in two days.

"Glass slices cleaner," she says. "Plus, my father will think the children cut themselves. If I use a knife, he'll suspect something." I hear the slight gasp of pain from my mother's lips. "I'll need samples from the girls, too. Combining all of our blood together will bind our powers."

What? I can't see, but I can hear liquid drip into a container. If she takes my blood, I will be marked for eternity. I can't let that happen. I'm trapped where I stand. If I move, they will see me. I'd been planning to run away for a few weeks now. I even confided with Tharin about it. *Oh no. My mother knows my plans.* The two of them probably have something cooked up already and are one step ahead of me. That must be why she's starting the ritual now. No matter where I go, she will be able to find me. I need to get out of here tonight.

It seems I'm not the only one with secrets to hide, though. Knowing that my mother and my beau have a scheme prepared—and that they don't want my grandfather to know—has me concerned. I don't dare attempt to confide with Tharin on anything I do from here on out, especially now. *I'm such a fool.*

In a low raspy voice, Mother says, "I'm going to find out who it is, Octavious. Now, you can either help me or stay out of my way."

Father grunts. "Now you're being dramatic." Of the two of them, he's always been the one who is reasonable.

"I'm being dramatic?"

"It's late, darling. Come to bed, and we can finish this in the morning," Father encourages her.

My parents casually walk down the dark, dreary hall to my sisters' room, passing me undetected.

"Rubbish," my mother protests. I notice she carries a silver tray containing the ritual items.

Coming out from my hiding spot, I keep a bit of distance from them, and my heart skips a beat when I hear them creak open the door. *She's following through with it.*

Moments later, I hear a slight discomfort coming from one of the twins. "Darling," I hear my father say, "do we have to do this now? Leave this nonsense behind, Sarmira. It can wait until Petra's birthday. Let the children sleep."

"Octavious, someone has suppressed her magic, and I'm going to find out whom."

"You don't know that for sure, Sarmira. You realize this could do more harm to them than good, don't you?"

Wait, I'm confused. I thought this was about my plans to run away but it sounds like this is much deeper than that.

Another whimper comes from my other sister.

"The children don't deserve this injustice because of your paranoia," my father argues.

"Tave, love, is that what you think? That I'm paranoid?"

"Look at you. Drawing blood from the children in the middle of the night!"

The moans from my sisters soften. They're ten years younger than me and will make very powerful necromancer witches, someday. As for me, I wish I never had such potential magic. I'm so fearful of it that I refuse to try this sort of sorcery. And love, well, you will never see that from my family. Here's the proof. My mother thinks that drawing blood from innocent children for her personal gain is no big deal.

She clucks her tongue. "Oh, darling, I know how this looks, but I also know someone else has interfered."

"Interfered in what? You know how you sound right now?"

My mother must be comforting my sisters to go back to sleep, or she would have been in my room already for my sample of blood. I need to think of something fast.

"Her magical powers will not come unless we unbind them," Mother persists.

"Unbind them? Sarmira, I thought you were binding the children together?" my father asks.

"I am, but before I can do that, I need to separate the magical spell that old woman cast on our eldest daughter years ago."

So, my mother knows about her? I wonder if she knows about the hidden items that were given to me by the old woman, too?

"Is that what this is all about? Your obsession that a harmless old woman gave our daughter a stone? Sarmira, it was just a rock."

I REMEMBER THAT DAY well...

My family and I were enjoying the ocean. I spotted on the beach an old woman sitting on a circle of driftwood weaving a dream catcher.

I wandered over to her. My parents didn't approve of me talking with strangers, and on this day, they were distracted with my twin sisters getting too close to the waves.

"Hello," I said. "Can I watch you weave? Those are very beautiful."

The old woman smiled. "These are soul catchers. Each one holds a different name, protecting those who own them, and prevents nightmares." The one she worked on had turquoise, blue, and pink threads intertwined with seashells.

My eyes widened. "Really?" I sat next to her and watched. "Can you teach me how to make one?"

"Perhaps another day, yes. I sense your parents would not approve." She turned, eyeing them on the shoreline, each cradling one of my sisters. They noticed our gazes, and my father put down Tia, the older of the two.

"Get away from her!" my father shouted. He ran toward us and the fear in his eyes frightened me.

"Looks like it's my time to go." She slipped a stone into my hand. "If you ever want to contact me again, this will guide your way." She chanted a few words, holding my hands, then disappeared with all her possessions, leaving behind one soul catcher and the stone.

My father reached me. "Are you okay?" Hugging me, he added, "Did she hurt you?"

"Dad, I'm fine, but you scared her away. I was just talking to her. That's all."

"Right." He took in a deep breath. "I thought we taught you better than that. Never talk to strangers." He looked at the ground and turned a full circle. "What was she doing anyway?"

"Weaving dream catchers," I said, confused. He didn't see the one at my feet.

"Come on, we're done for the day." Clasping my hand to his, he tugged me up from sitting on the log, but not before I grabbed the soul catcher the old woman left behind.

The funny thing about that memory of the past is that I've had nightmares since.

THE OLD WOMAN. MY mother is going to find her, and when she does... devastation will follow. If anyone defies her, Mother will make her presence known. Oh, I don't want to think about that. I need to warn the old woman, but I must be careful. Question is, how?

A loud horn blares, bringing me back from my reverie. I duck back into the shadows, knowing my parents will be flying out of my sisters' room in seconds.

"What in all of Elleirodal is going on?" my mother cries.

12

2

GRANDFATHER'S WRATH

T HE COMMOTION GIVES ME ample opportunity to slide quietly back into my room undetected. I'm not sticking around. I need to run away as fast as possible. Something tells me my fate depends on it. I pull out my bag from under the bed and fill it with essentials. I also place the mysterious book I stole, along with the plans, inside it. Something is amiss, and I'm going to take advantage of the chaos. Nothing new, though, there's always some sort of drama surfacing.

But this time, my mother is involved, which means this drama will explode at some point. After hearing the gossip this evening, my senses tell me something sinister is upon us. The conversation between my mother and Tharin and her plans to bind my powers with hers and the twins has me taking flight. It's not normal for a mother to be so power-hungry.

And Tharin, my heart breaks thinking about it. I thought he loved me. Our relationship is a lie. This whole time, us sneaking about the castle for a kiss here and there, it was all a pre-planned attempt to capture my heart. Well, he did a number on it for sure. I won't be that damsel in distress. If he thinks I'm that kind of girl, then he obviously doesn't know me that well. The promise of marriage and a better life, all for what? To get me in his bed? I'll be the last person he'll want to see the next time we meet up.

I still don't understand why my mother pushed us together. That I'll soon figure out, too, I'm sure. All I need is a strategy to weasel their game out of him.

On my birthday, I'll be forced to choose a side, good or evil, to lay the foundation to practice magic. No longer will I be a young girl, but a woman with purpose, duty, and responsibilities. Why do I have to choose anyway? Because of some sort of ancient tradition? The tradition that apparently my mother is attempting to get a head start on.

I'm not ready to be in line for the throne, nor will I ever be. I don't want this.

My parents have encouraged me several times to welcome in the darkness, but I've always pushed it away. Because of that, my magic isn't as powerful as most girls my age. Usually, by now, I'd be into dark magic and prepping for the ritual that will come on my birthday. I think they've had it with my denial of dark magic, though. They've locked me behind the castle doors for the last month, attempting to prepare me. If I compromise just once, there's no recovering from the innocence lost. For my first dark ritual assignment, I'm to take an innocent soul. Their essence. I've skated by thus far, but I know those days are numbered. And then, I'll forever be molded to the dark side. I've seen it happen with one of my father's brothers—Uncle Artan. We were close and grew up together. He was more like a brother to me, and we were the same age, too. I haven't seen him since that horrific day.

I look out the window above my bedframe, seeing nothing but pitch blackness. It won't be easy to climb out of it, but there isn't any other way to leave without my parents knowing. I'm going to need light, for the moon will not give me such a gift tonight. I know one of the perks of turning eighteen is I'll acquire nocturnal sight, but that doesn't help me now. I hear the slight howl of the wind as it escapes through the cracks of my window frame, indicating that it's frigid outside.

I hear glass break outside my door, and it startles me, so I hide my bag back under the bed.

Someone pounds on my door. "Get up!" A guard I imagine. I'm guessing it's the chaos catching up to me. Not another battle, I hope. The last one caught us off guard. I'm sick of battles. I look over to my nightstand and see it's three in the morning. *The witching hour.*

My locked door rattles. "Open up." The voice on the others side is muffled. "Petra, it's me."

It's Zia, my other twin sister. "What's going on?" Both of my sisters can be annoying but she's the milder of the two. Tia can be vindictive.

"It's Grandfather, and he said to come immediately."

"What is he doing here?"

"No idea, he just showed up minutes ago."

"Is that what all the madness is about?"

"Yeah, and he's furious. You better hurry and get downstairs. He's asking for you." Zia rushes away, leaving me in my room alone. This isn't like him to show up unannounced. I hope this doesn't impede my plans.

I decide to dress because the thought of coming down in my nightclothes feels weird to me, aside from the fact that I plan to flee anyway, so it's one less thing I need to do.

Before I get two feet outside my door, I hear more whispering. This time, I can't make out what they're saying. When I pass by, I see it's a couple of servants. The look in their eyes tells me they're afraid.

My twin sisters are not in their rooms when I trot past their door, and neither are my mother and father in theirs. As usual, I'm the last to arrive for any event.

I reach the top of the terrace leading to the open courtyard below. It's the center of our living quarters. Luscious green ivy covers the pillars in each corner, with a wraparound balcony at all four points of the square. The upper levels lead to perspective bed chambers, while the lower floor leads to various living spaces. There are two sets of staircases on opposite sides of the square, one on the north wing and one on the south. I can hear my grandfather shouting from the parlor. "I trusted you, Sarmira, and this is how you repay me?"

Slowly I ascend the stairs from the south side of the courtyard, listening quietly to their arguing. Coming into a room in the middle of a shouting match doesn't sit well with me. I know how this will end. So, which one of us will die tonight? There isn't a servant in sight, and that goes without saying because they, too, know.

As I step down off my last step, Tharin glides through the front doors with his back to me. His attire looks perfect as always, and not a hair out of place. He slips into the parlor, saying, "You wanted to see me, your majesty?"

Quietly, I follow behind and stand near the door frame, unnoticed. Everyone inside the room looks either tired or frightened.

Grandfather's lips curl with disgust. "There you are. Have a seat." Anger glints in his eyes at the sheer presence of Tharin, but my grandfather remains cool as always.

My heart skips a beat. Both from seeing Tharin and the anger in my grandfather's eyes. Deep in my soul, I know something is wrong. I've not seen him this angry in years. The last time he was this enraged was the day we returned from the beach and my father confessed to seeing the old woman. I swear the only reason my father lives today was that we kids were witnesses to grandfather's tirade.

Both my parents come from a long line of dark witchcraft. All my ancestors dealt with dark magic in one form or another. I've seen its power firsthand. But I also saw the sacrifices it cost to get there.

Tharin's eyes dart around, and he looks nervous.

"Father, what's this all about? The roosters aren't even up." My mother appears relaxed as always. No one ever knows her emotions—she hides them well. Except for me. I can see the hint of suspicion in her eyes.

He ignores her question. "Where is Petra?"

I jump at my name. Fear captures my soul. "I'm right here, Grandfather." I hurry into the room.

His mannerisms calm and I stiffen, watching him look me up and down as though I've been doing something unscrupulous. "What took you so long?"

"Well, I wasn't about to come down in my night clothes." Clearly, he can see I've dressed, as though we're about to receive guests, while the rest of the household is still in their nightcaps.

"Ah, you see?" He points at me while staring hard at the rest of the family. "She will be your new queen someday." He glares at my mother. "Sarmira, I had high hopes for you. I really thought the marriage between you and Octavious would lighten your heart, but it's only darkened it more."

"Father, whatever are you talking about?" she protests. "You come into our quarters in the middle of the night and expect us all to dress for you?" She shoots me a look full of distaste.

I know that look. It's her *I'll deal with you later* look. How is this my fault?

"I know what you and Tharin have been planning." He peers deep into my mother's eyes.

I watch her shiver. It isn't obvious, but I've never seen Mother show fear. She stumbles upon her words. "I—I haven't any idea what you're talking about," she lies.

"Are you going to stand here and pretend that you didn't have the scheme to take the first-born heir of our line and have her fall in love with an imposter and have him impregnate her, knowing that she would be ruined? That the marriage between her and her betrothed, Edmond, would be null and void?"

Mother's face goes sheet white. Her eyes burn with fury. I know that look, too. This won't end well. I don't know whether to scream at her or thank her. Sure, she devised this plan and it angers me, but what angers me more is I was on the receiving end of this charade.

"You!" She stares at Tharin. "We had a deal."

"M—Madame, what are you talking about?"

I smirk. Does he play my mother for a fool? I know she can see right through him. Tharin steps back as if to anticipate her next move. "I assure you, Sire—" he looks to my grandfather— "I've no idea what she is talking about." He puts up his hands in defense of my mother's advances.

"Lies!" Without warning, she forms a fireball in her palm and strikes him with such force that he incinerates before our very eyes.

I'm in utter shock. I want to puke, and my heart is crushed. I know I should be angry at both of them, but I hadn't had the chance to confront Tharin. "Why kill him, Mother?" I need to stay calm and pretend I see nothing wrong with her actions.

"He was worthless, Petra," she says, trying to justify her reasons.

My grandfather grunts, while my father looks for a hiding servant to clean up the ashes of Tharin left on the marble tiles.

Nobody seems to care about how I feel. Still, I fight back the tears that I know will be a sentence for torture should I show any emotion.

"Well, now that that's cleared up," my grandfather says. "We can continue matters." He glares at my mother. "Sarmira, I bind your powers." He snaps his fingers as though that's all he needs to do. No spell, no ritual, nothing but the click of his fingers.

Mother screams in anger. "You can't be serious, Father."

"Keep it up, and I'll bind them forever."

Grandfather directs his attention to me. "Your birthday is in two days, my dear grandchild, you need your rest." His gentle tone crawls under my skin as if nothing ever happened. "Go, get out of here. I'll have guards set outside your door to make sure no one disturbs you so you can get your beauty sleep. Your wedding will commence as planned."

Not if I have anything to say about it. I can hardly breathe. I feel like my heart has been ripped from my chest. I will not marry my betrothed. Not now, not ever.

I realize now Tharin was after power and the inheritance of what marriage would bring. He never loved me. It appears my mother's plans were to foil the arranged marriage between Edmond and me, destroying my role as heir.

She also knew it would cause a war among the factions of the underworld. I think back to when Tharin was in my grandfather's study and sprinkled glitter like dust upon the drawer and floor. Who was he, really? I mean, the way we met I thought was by chance. I knew Tharin would never be more than a lover, and I would still have to marry Edmond. No, I know that, too, is a lie. Edmond is from the western part of the underworld and Tharin the east. Grandfather controls both the northern and southern realms, which are larger. Therefore, he holds the superior shares. If his kingdoms were overcome, say someone else—I look over at Mother, her face flushed with fury—would take control. I'm beginning to see, yes, she wants all the power for herself, but Tharin's realm held a wavering significance. Would it have been enough to overturn Grandfather? What would she gain by crossing her father? And now, Tharin is dead.

I know my destiny. I remember the dreams, and I've seen things. Horrifying things. I vow to change that. It's the only option I have.

I must move on as planned and get as far away from them as I can, for if I'm caught at any point, they will not hesitate to kill me.

This revelation spurs my motivation. I will flee tonight.

3

ESCAPE INTO DARKNESS

T HE GUARDS WALK ME to my room and then stand post outside my door. Escape might be a bit more difficult now, but I'm not going to let that stop me.

Taking full advantage of my grandfather's tirade, I use this time to devise my getaway. He doesn't know I'm about to run away, of course, but I do find the situation a bit ironic.

Pulling my bag back from under my bed, I continue to stuff it with my most important belongings, including my journal. It's more like a diary than anything, but it has recipes of different spells, as well as a calendar of the lunar phases. Which reminds me... I look out the window, thinking this is good news, because not only is the moon dark, but my mother's magic has been bound, allowing me ample opportunity to slip within the shadows undetected. However, it's a double edge sword, for there will be lack of nighttime visibility.

The frigid temperatures remind me that this attempt to flee will be difficult. I change into wool trousers and a sweater. My coat, on the other hand, is downstairs in the dining hall. I can't risk going after it, but I do have a heavy cloak that my Uncle Artan gave me as a premature birthday gift a few months ago before he was forced to choose a side. The day before his death, in fact. He told me to wear it the day I turn eighteen and said not to tell my parents it was from him. I've kept it hidden under my bed this entire time. Of course, I couldn't wait until my birthday, so I opened it that night.

I guess it's only fitting that I wear it now. I take it out of the square box. The garment is wrapped in a protective covering with the note still attached. Tears form as I open the delicate envelope.

My Dearest Petra,

I hope that you will enjoy this gift. Don't forget to read the care instructions.

He doesn't sign the note. I imagine it's for fear of being identified.

I pull the protective covering off the cloak and shake out the wrinkles. It's navy blue, and it has a beautiful white inlay stitching on the front collar. It also looks warm.

Swinging the cloak around my shoulders, I immediately feel something magical. It isn't anything I can explain, but I feel rejuvenated like this garment must have some sort of magical element to it, but what, I'm not sure. I spontaneously tuck my hands into my pockets and glance at the mirror in my room, catching my reflection. What I see has me nearly letting out a scream loud enough for a guard to burst through the door. Thankfully, I swallow my surprise. *How is this possible?*

Stepping closer to the mirror, I still cannot believe what I am seeing—that is, what I'm not seeing. My reflection has vanished.

I pull the cloak off my shoulders, still feeling pure wonder. As I hold the cloak in my hands, it looks like any ordinary cloth, and when I test my eyes once more by putting the cape back on, my entire body disappears.

"How clever you are, Uncle Artan," I say under my breath.

I've heard of such items as these, but in our part of the world, it was always rumored as a myth. Clearly, invisible cloaks do exist. It has me wondering how he got a hold of one, which reminds me to look for the signature label. I check the stitching and find nothing and then move my fingers to the inside pocket of the garment. The first one is empty, but when I slip my hand into the other one, my fingers touch something within, and I pull out a note. Unfolding the paper, it reads:

This cloak is weaved with a magical language stitched into the fabric. Those who wear it will feel the effects. Handle with care.

I grin, chuckling, because I discovered what it does before reading the instructions. I return the note.

Looking up at my window, I rethink my strategy, as the frame is small. *Who am I kidding?* I take in a deep breath, feeling relieved that I won't have to escape through the small window above my bedframe.

I fluff my pillows and arrange them to give the illusion I'm in the bed sleeping. My heart races, because although this cloak will conceal me, there is still a great fear that I might be caught. I test the theory that anything I carry will also become hidden, so I haul my bag over my shoulder to confirm my assumptions and look in the mirror.

The sound of my boots will be a dead giveaway. I take them off and tie the laces together and sling them around my shoulders. I do a once over of my room, double-checking if I've missed anything that would be essential, and realize I forgot to grab a few protective stones. Black tourmaline and labradorite. Both will protect me in different ways.

My bedroom door will be the first hurdle to pass because it creaks when opening. The guards outside my door will know immediately. There have been plenty of times invisible shifters have tried to make their way past Grandfather's army undetected. How will I pull this one off? I need a distraction. Fierce winds outside catch my attention, and I glance at my window. I raise a brow. *Perfect.*

I climb my way up to the frame to open the glass. A rush of cold air brushes past me. It's going to be a cold walk to the safety of the forest beyond. Snowflakes smack my face, making me shiver. The flurries alert me that it's much colder than I first anticipated. Pushing the glass open as wide as possible, I jump back down off my bed and attempt to carry out my plan to get past the guards. Gently, I pull at the knob of my bedroom door and allow the wind to do the rest.

As predicted, the two guards push the entrance open farther to investigate, and I use the opportunity to slip out unnoticed. I fear that if they find that it's pillows under my covers and not me, it will be more difficult to escape the palace.

Even though I hide under this marvelous cloak unseen, a part of me still has some reservations that I won't be able to pull off the impossible. Getting past all the sentries will be difficult.

My grandfather. A thought crosses my mind that he will see right through my façade. Is he still downstairs?

It's been an hour since he called the family down for the horrid lecture, and the castle feels quiet. I can hear my father snore as I pass my parents' room.

Quietly, I continue forward until I reach the central courtyard in our living quarters. My grandfather has his head down on one of the patio tables, snoring, with half a glass of ale next to him. All the doors to every entrance are shut tight with a guard at each post. How am I going to get out of this? I cannot leave unless a door opens.

If I don't think of something fast, the guards in my room will discover my disappearance.

A horn blares.

Too late.

My grandfather wakes, and the sentries who were guarding my doors call, "My Lord, the princess is gone."

4

TRAPPED

"WHAT DO YOU MEAN the princess is gone? Which one?" my grandfather demands.

The noise and chaos wakes the household and I shiver, thinking at any moment I'm going to get caught. I hide against the wall near the front gate of the courtyard, observing the servants rushing, the guards on alert, and my father turning three shades of red. Hesitation grabs me, and I have the urge to wimp out until the thoughts of this evening's escapades cross my mind once more. Tharin's death is the beginning of something I want no part of.

My mother storms into the room. "What is the meaning of this disruption now? Father, this is twice you've woken my entire family. Can we not have a peaceful sleep?" *She hasn't realized I've disappeared.*

My grandfather scowls, putting up a hand to stop her ranting. "Go on, Oscar."

The guard eyes my mother before answering. "Petra."

Mother steps closer. "What about Petra?" Her face shows shock, worry, and anger all at once.

"That is what I'm trying to find out." My grandfather's face grows stern. "Are you sure?" he asks Oscar.

Oscar fumbles his words in response. I honestly don't blame him. Both my grandfather and mother can be unpredictable. "Her window has been left open and her bed not slept in."

A low rumble sounds deep within my grandfather's throat, followed by my mother fleeing down the corridors toward our living quarters, calling out my name.

My grandfather ignores my mother's theatrics, saying, "The drop alone would kill Petra. No, I don't believe she's run away. Tracks in the snow would be a clear indicator of that. Did you check the perimeter?"

The snow. I haven't thought this through. I almost let out a moan of frustration. How am I going to avoid my tracks?

Both guards look at each other. Another huff of annoyance passes through my grandfather's lips. "Search the castle. She's in here somewhere. There is no way she could escape the guarded doors."

My heart sinks. I need to find a way out of here fast. I look toward the entrance. If only they would open the doors. I fear through the chaos someone might bump into me, so I manage to tuck myself behind the entry table that sits to the right of the entrance doors and hide.

Another horn blasts through the castle walls. The same horn that alerts the fortress of possible attacks, is used to warn Grandfather's army now—only it's a hunt to find me. I try to keep as still as stone while the guards and servants flurry about the palace looking for my whereabouts.

After what seems like an eternity later, Oscar comes into the room again. "Your Majesty, we've searched everywhere. She isn't here."

Grandfather grunts. "Keep looking. She couldn't have gotten far." He turns to the guards standing post at the entrance to the outer courtyard. My exit for escape. "Check the outside boundaries of the fortress," my grandfather bellows and orders the entrance opened.

My heart pounds. *Yes, now is my chance.* I sneak behind the guards but not too close. I haven't any idea if this cloak's invisibility will hold up should someone bump into me. I stand only a few feet behind them. As they pass through the doors, they're quickly shut, narrowly missing me.

The brisk cold weather bites as I enter the outer center courtyard. The snow has made its way through the square, blanketing the cobblestone with a white layer. They will see my prints in the snow if I move. My boots are still strung around my neck, and my feet grow numb, standing on the icy bricks, but if I try to head for cover now, one of the guards will notice. This is going to force me to cluster closer to the guards lining up for the outer gates. My heart races. Everyone knows a necromancer can hear the beating of a panicked heart. Grandfather especially. How am I to keep calm in chaos such as this? Unless the cloak can hide that, too?

The lead lieutenant carries out orders to the rest of the men and raises the outer gates. This is my chance to get out. I follow behind the last soldier and skip away just outside the castle fortress, but I'm not safe until I reach the main gate where the drawbridge leads outside the palace grounds.

Above me, lining the wall walk, archers ready their bows looking out beyond the castle barriers. *Do they have orders to kill me?* I feel trapped. The sun will rise soon which will make it easier to see my tracks in the snow, and with so many guards on high alert, the time is now to slither away into the darkness.

I spot a wagon near the west entrance. A team of horses are hitched for travel. *That's my out.*

Keeping vigilant and eyeing every possible guard that might glance my way, I inch slowly to the tail end of the vendor's wagon. It's too full to crawl inside. Hoping I have enough strength to hold on with my fingers growing numb, I hop onto the carriage rim just in time before the driver slaps the reins and the horses jerk forward. *Guess this is one way to avoid tracks in the snow.*

This gives me a spare moment to slip on my shoes. My feet are so cold I can't feel my toes.

I begin to tie my laces when I hear the woman sitting atop the cart ask, "What do you suppose is going on?"

"I don't know, but it might delay our plans if we don't leave now, darling," her companion, says.

The team advances toward the entrance and two guards stop the wagon.

"And where are you two going on such a cold, blustering early morning?" one guard asks.

"Traveling to the next town over to deliver supplies," the merchant says.

"Not without a search." The other guard pulls the blankets back hiding the merchandise inside the cart. They do a thorough check before giving the merchant approval to leave.

"Is everything all right, sir?" the merchant asks.

"Fine. We're looking for a fugitive."

Fugitive? So, that's what I am now?

"Why are you leaving in such freezing conditions?" a guard presses.

"Well, if you must know, my wife's sister is ill and she needs medicine."

The guard nods. "Carry on, you're free to go." He alerts the sentries to lift the drawbridge.

I hitch a ride for a good thirty minutes, and despite the minimal light from the dark moon, the snow still manages to lighten the way. Even so, the travel across the vast snowy fields will be difficult. The snow is deep, and the roads are not much better.

I look up and watch the flakes fall onto my face, and smile, knowing this may be an asset. The snow will cover my tracks. I tie my laces that I'd forgotten to do earlier, and tuck extra cloth around the edges of my boots to avoid the snow from getting inside my boots before hopping off my ride.

I do hope those poor folks reach their destination, but that's not my concern now, and I ease my way into the dark. I need to get as far away from here as possible.

5

TRACKS IN THE SNOW

MY MOTHER TOLD ME my nocturnal sight becomes more powerful the closer I get to my birthday. I sure wish it would kick in because I feel like I'm walking blind. I adjust to the atmosphere as I look around. If only the moon wasn't so dark.

I look back toward the road, noticing the set of footprints I leave behind, and I'm concerned that it will lead Grandfather right to me. The wind howls fiercely, and the frozen flurries brush across my face. I'm freezing, and I can't feel my fingers because it's so cold, but I know the alternative isn't an option. I choose freedom, so I press onward toward the safety of the thick forest that lines parallel with the roadside. Hopefully,

I'll find shelter within the branches of the trees. I thought about continuing my walk along the road, but if Grandfather's soldiers travel down the same path, they might see my footprints. At least if I veer off the route slightly, I can hide my tracks easier. The outline of the forest, motivates me to push forward despite my aching limbs. I need shelter before I freeze to death.

Something I didn't count on was food. I'd not packed anything to eat. Nothing in this vast wilderness will supply sustenance for the hunger pangs invading my stomach. Despite these shortcomings, I will push myself and find my way through the thick forest. I won't let a little snow stop me.

It's been so long since I was in these woods. How will I find her? Once it's calmer, I'll continue to the blue oak tree where I hid the stone deep in the ground. My hope is it's still where I left it. Maybe the rock she gave me will lead the way.

My mind wanders as I tread through the snow to avoid dwelling on the pain and numbness in my fingers and toes. Thinking about the old woman I met on the beach when I was thirteen, I realize I never found out her name.

I remember the old woman whispering in my ear, "I bind your powers to this rock. Keep it with you always. When you're ready for the magic to come, look to the stone to call upon the raven at midday."

Hopefully, when I find my hidden rock, I'll find the old woman. I buried the soul catcher, too. I didn't want to take the chance of anyone finding either of them. I think I made a mistake by not listening to her, though.

The words my mother spouted earlier imprint on my mind and has me wondering if this old woman did indeed bind my powers. But how would Mother know? She wasn't anywhere around when it happened.

It was a week before my thirteenth birthday. The first rite of passage in our family bloodline. I wonder if that has something to do with why Mother wanted to combine our blood. Is this the reason why I could never do magic like the rest of my family? I haven't the powers like them. Nothing flows to my fingers, igniting with flames, or creating something out of nothing such as food, water, or items. I can't conjure, or cast a spell, or create any sort of magic from any of the elements. Mother tells me I've been cursed. Through the last five years, I've learned to make up for it by reading books and writing spells in my journal. Maybe someday it will be useful. There must be a reason why the old woman bound my powers.

We've not been to the beach since. The same day we met the old woman is the same day I hid the stone in a hollowed-out blue oak tree. I knew it was something to cherish. I didn't dare keep it in the castle. My mother would have found it, so I buried it.

That night at our campsite, I scurried down the path to the ocean—it was a full moon night, so visibility it wasn't as minimal as tonight. I spotted a blue oak tree, rooted along the oceanside cliff at the edge of the thick forest. It glowed a beautiful shade of cobalt blue with silver sparkles that looked like glitter gleaming in the moonlight. I was enchanted to see such a stunning sight. When I investigated further, I found a hollow opening big enough for an adult to fit inside, so there I hid the stone along with the soul catcher. I wanted to hide it where no one would suspect it to be. It was that night, while holding the stone before burying it in the soft ground, that I was given a glimpse of the future. It terrified me, and I never looked back until today.

Each step takes me deeper into the woods. I'm still knee-deep in the snow though, and the shelter from the tree limbs is not shielding me as well as I had anticipated. I must go until the soil meets the snow to lose my tracks.

The blue oak tree is much farther out than the protection of the woods. I must pass through the forest to the other side to reach the ocean, but I'm beginning to feel exhausted.

The snow begins to lighten, and I glance back, realizing my tracks are still visible, leaving a trace of my existence behind. A hint of orange and yellow peeks out along the horizon. The sun will crest soon. Relief settles in me, knowing I will be able to see much easier.

A raven swoops down in front of me and stares. It moves its head and then lets out a deep caw. I see its eyes glow a slight blue. I'm surprised I can see the bird as dark as it is. "What are you trying to tell me?" I whisper. It takes flight, disappearing through the winter sky. Is this the raven the old woman mentioned? It's not midday.

My legs hurt and begin to throb, but I keep moving. I must find shelter. "Just a few more steps," I whisper to myself. I could really use a good fire about now.

I'm about to give up and let the cold snow take me when I look up to see flecks of light.

The closer they approach the more enchanted I become. They look like fireflies.

My breathing is labored, and I'm too tired to appreciate the beauty. I sink to my knees and collapse. I can't move any farther. I have no more energy. I lie in the snow, and I stare up at the sky, watching the blending of the fireflies that mix with the falling snowflakes surrounding me. There are so many of them. The buzzing sounds invade my ears, but I haven't the strength to shoo them away. "Please, I mean you no harm."

They glow in an array of colors and begin to multiply, coming by the thousands and hovering all around. I've heard of such creatures but never have I witnessed them with my own eyes.

It doesn't take me long to discover they are trying to help.

I feel my body lift off the ground, and I look down, watching them cover my tracks.

Hovering in the air a couple feet above the snow, they carry me across the vast snowy forest.

I hope these fiery friends are leading me to safety. They'd hardly help me if they were taking me to my demise, right? I'm carried quite far, longer than I expected, and soon I begin to hear the sounds of the ocean. It's hard to see through the thick flakes, but in the distance, something glows a bright blue. Can it be the blue oak tree? The closer we approach the brighter the light.

I'm finally set on solid ground. "Thank you," I say. The relief of feeling safe pushes away the fear of my family finding me.

I look ahead, seeing the bright blue oak tree, and realize the premonition that was shown to me from the rock I buried all those years ago has just come true tonight.

6

THE BLUE OAK TREE

LONG BRANCHES COVER THE hollow opening, but I recognize this to be the tree because of the carving on the trunk. The symbol is as I remember. An oval shape centered on top of a square shape with lines traveling to each corner like a spiderweb. At the time, I didn't know what it was, but as I look closer, I realize this is a light witch symbol. A protection spell to prevent anyone or anything from coming in close contact with the tree. I remember the premonition revealing this.

I push back the brush and place my palm on the circle. I don't know why I know this, but something within me compels me to do it. The symbol glows a slight blue, and the tree reveals a hollow opening. Venturing inside, I watch as the hole reseals, leaving me in darkness. Seconds later, a light appears, and I realize a single whisp has followed me inside.

"Have you come to keep me company?" I whisper, as if the tiny creature can reply.

The whisp buzzes around our closed enclosure and lands on a mushroom growing from the inside walls of the trunk. I look closer and discover this tiny whisp is actually a fairy.

I smile. "Well, aren't you full of surprises?" I set my bag down and sit.

She doesn't speak, but I see her smile and nod.

The fairy uses her magic and sets a stein down, along with bread and jam, next to me.

My stomach growls looking at the food. "You must be a conjuring fairy."

The fairy presses me to eat it.

I smile. "Thank you. I am a bit hungry." I take the bread without hesitation and wash it down with water.

Once I finish, the dishes disappear. "You're too kind. How can I ever thank you?"

I look around the small space, and it's as I remember it. The ground is soft, and the area is cozy. Remarkably warmer than the outside weather, too. "I wonder if you can help me?" I ask, looking at the tiny fairy fluttering in front of my nose. "I've come for something I hid long ago."

The fairy nods.

"Do you know where it is? I've forgotten the exact spot."
I search the floor in the carved-out space and dig in the area
I think I buried my treasures.

The fairy begins to buzz again and settles in a spot near
my hands. "Are you trying to tell me to dig here?"

She nods.

I do as the fairy suggests.

As I dig, I begin to feel something solid. I dig some more
until the tiny container I had buried years ago reveals the
top of its lid. "Thank you, my friend."

I pull the box from the soil and brush off the dirt. It is a
brown leatherbound case with gold trim.

I huff, remembering when I buried it. It was the next
morning, and I snuck out of the tent early. I'd taken my
mother's jewelry box, dumped the gems in the sand, and
scouted for a place to hide my new treasures. When Mother found her jewelry case missing, she was furious. She
suspected goblins took it. I didn't dare tell her the truth.
Who brings jewelry with them while camping anyway? Of
course, I didn't know the importance of valuable gems, as
I do now.

The fairy buzzes about, bringing me back from my reverie.

"The key." I look at the tiny fairy, and she doesn't appear
worried. "I can't open it. I think it's locked."

The fairy darts into the keyhole and disappears. At first, I think something happened to her, but to my surprise, she pops open the lid.

I laugh in delight. "You're quite the clever one, aren't you? I appreciate your help."

Inside, my container is just as I left it. I'm relieved to find my items are still here. The soul catcher that I hid from my parents and the rock. I examine the black stone the old woman gave me and take a closer look. I notice there are a few faint yellow lines flowing through it. If I shine what little light I have in this dark space, I can see a slight hint of blue. I tuck the stone into my pocket and bring out my other stones—the black tourmaline and labradorite—placing them in the box, and stuff it in my bag.

I take a deep breath. "Shall we get some sleep?"

The fairy flutters around and then provides a warm blanket and pillow. "How remarkable. Thank you again."

Her body twinkles a bit, and her glowing aura brightens as she circles above my head before settling back on the spongy mushroom she was on before. She sits, watching me settle into a cozy cocoon of warmth before turning out her light.

7

THE RAVEN

I WAKE IN DARKNESS, but I can see the sunlight peeking through parts of the hollow tree, plus the fairy still sleeps upon her mushroom bed and she sends a slight glow of light.

There are sounds of birds singing beyond the protective barrier, but I can tell the snow has deepened from earlier this morning, because the crackling of ice pings, and the snap of melting snow chimes my ears. I hear a snow owl hoot and it startles me.

Picking up the stone hiding in my cloak, I examine again the swirls of color it weaves. I've no idea what kind of rock it is, but it's beautiful with the vibrant blues, yellows, and greens intertwining together. Depending on the angle of light, the stone changes color.

The fairy begins to stir. Her wings buzz.

"Good morning. Did you sleep well?" I ask.

She yawns, stretches her arms, and quickly flutters upward in the air.

I smile at the small creature buzzing about.

Her wings flutter back and forth as fast as a hummingbird, and her face looks like any other human except her ears are pointed and her nose, too. When she speaks, she chirps like a bird.

"I'm sorry, I don't know what you're trying to say."

She comes closer, landing on the open lid of the jewelry box and sings some more.

"I do wish I could understand you," I say.

She flutters in circles, then disappears into thin air, followed by a burst of light. Sparkling dust hails down upon me, and I cover my head with my hands. She reappears my size, saying, with a smile, "Can you understand me now?"

"Oh my," I say, nodding in amazement. "How did you do that?"

"I'm a Fae. Fairies don't normally shapeshift."

"Oh, I didn't know that." Even at human size, she still has a glow. "I'm Petra."

She giggles. "I know who you are, silly."

Amazed at her answer, I reply, "You do?"

"Of course. My whole city knows about you." She sits down. "I'm Sylvie. The Fae leader of the forest."

"Those fireflies that lifted me to safety, were they Fae, too?"

She giggles. "They were. My army of fireflies if you want to call them that."

"You mean, you could see me under this invisible cloak?"

"Of course, I'm a Fae. You can't hide from a Fae. We're always watching. It's our enchantments that made the cloak magical in the first place."

The care instructions come to mind, and I reach into the inside pocket, pull it out, and re-read it. "The stitching. It's a spell written in your language, isn't it?"

Sylvie smiles. "Very intuitive."

I tilt my head in wonder. "It's been a long time since I've been inside this tree. How did you know?"

"I was here the day you buried the treasure. You didn't notice me because I hid above you. At first, I was startled, then I watched what you had in your possession and knew immediately who you encountered."

Surprised by her confession, I ask, "Do you know her name?"

"I do not. We refer to her as the Eye of the Raven."

"Oh?" The raven that swooped down before my feet during the early morning, comes to mind. "*The*... Eye of the Raven. So, the myth is true?" I'd heard the stories... rumors really that she saved the eastern territories from the brink of war.

47

She became a legend, but that was so long ago, that it was forgotten.

"She's the protector of this realm. And when I saw you had the soul catcher and the stone that accompanied it, I knew you were under her protection."

"Her protection?" What an odd thing to say. I wonder if this Fae knows how to find her.

"This is my home. One of many hollow trees in our forest," she goes on. "It's the first hollow blue oak tree before entering the Hollow Forest. You came into our woods from the west side. Where we are now, is the east."

"It makes sense why people call it the Hollow Forest. I always thought it was because there was a hollow opening to the black void. My father would tell me never to enter because those who do never come back."

"He's right. Those that enter never return," Sylvie, confirms.

I shudder at her validation. "Am I your prisoner?" The thought of being held captive sends panic through my veins. I've no magical powers to protect myself.

"No silly, we're here to guide you to the protection of Wisteria Keep."

"Wisteria Keep?"

"You'll see. We better get going if we want to get to the gate on time." Before I have time to press with more questions, she transforms into a fairy—um Fae—and buzzes around once more.

I stuff my trinkets into my bag and sling it over my back, saying, "Shall we move forward?"

With my hat on my head, gloves on my hands, and a warm cloak slung around my shoulders, I'm ready for the wintery wonderland beyond the hollow tree that has magically protected me from the elements.

The Fae flutters a bit more and then brings down the barrier, exposing us to the bitter cold. She flies off, disappearing into a blanket of white forested trees.

"Wait, you're going too fast." I run after her, but it is no use. She's gone. "See you later, I guess... thanks for your help."

THE MORNING IS TOO quiet, making me feel a little uneasy. Another layer of snow blankets the ground, which makes it more difficult to walk. I pull the stone from my pocket and peer at the shiny object. I remember the old woman's words again. *"When you're ready for the magic to lead the way, call upon the raven at midday."*

I look up at the sky and can clearly see it isn't the afternoon yet. Still morning by a few hours. I trudge through the snow and work my way deeper into the forest. I'm still not out of danger from my parents seeking my whereabouts. I'm sure of that. However, I'm a little relieved that they will have a hard time tracing my tracks now, thanks to the Fae. My mother will go to any lengths to get me back into her clutches, though, so I need to tread lightly.

A week before my birthday, she warned this day would come. That I would have to embrace the dark side of magic. The stunt she pulled the previous night was a stark reminder of what she'll do to increase her power, and it sends chills down my spine. One more day. Tomorrow at the stroke of midnight, I will turn eighteen and must choose a side. Normally I don't run from my problems but staying would have been much worse.

Tharin must have known this, too. I wish I knew his real motive, and it hurts thinking about it, but she took his life so I may never know the truth. Not that he would be honest with me anyway.

If the old woman can hide well among the necromancer witches of the underworld, then perhaps I can live with her. I'm doubtful she'll allow that, though, but she did give me this stone. Question is, was it just a childhood gift or a gesture to gain my parents' favor? Whatever it was, I can tell that this stone has much more meaning than your average rock.

A snow owl releases a territorial call in the treetops, startling me. It's probably the same one that hooted earlier.

Hours pass slowly, and I feel like I'm spinning in circles. The bitter cold crawls through the protective clothing I wear, and I'm starting to think this stone I carry in my palm doesn't work.

I'm deep in the forest, lost, and haven't any food. I'm going to starve to death. Perhaps I'm a fool for thinking I'd find a witch that carries such unique magic, but I can't give up.

"It's about midday, so where is this raven?" I ask myself.

There's a cawing response behind me. I turn to see a beautiful black bird land a few feet away.

I've heard of such creatures that hang out in groups. It's said that when you see many together, it means the Crow Man is near. Fear fills my mind, but when I look closer, I notice this bird has stark crystal-blue eyes. I have a distinct sense it's the same raven from yesterday. I've never seen such a magnificent creature up so close before. It's bigger than a crow, and its tail and beak are curved. I look around to see none of its friends have accompanied it. "You're not any ordinary blackbird, are you?" I ask as if it will respond.

Its low caw tells me this bird isn't a crow at all, but a raven. The fact that it doesn't have black eyes should have been my first clue, although ravens don't have blue eyes either.

Could this be the legendary Eye of the Raven? Preposterous. Leaving the idea behind, I press on, seeking a path that will possibly lead me away from my doom and the direction of a better life.

The bird flies off, and although I don't know why, something inside me says to pursue it.

As though on cue, the stone in my palm lights up. If I veer in the wrong direction, the blue glow dims, and if I veer in the right direction, it brightens. Like a compass, I'm able to track the bird, and it leads me out of the dark, snowy forest. I run to keep up, and I'm lured to the edge of a ravine and slip, almost falling to my death, but I catch onto a branch that manages to hold my weight, stopping me from plummeting.

I sit to catch my breath. "That was close."

Peering down, the ravine looks endless. There's a slight hint that water might be flowing at the bottom, but either way, nobody would survive such a fall as that. I look down at my closed fist and open it. The stone still glows bright. I've managed to hang onto the precious object. I'm close to my journey's end, and I feel like I'm not alone. I turn my head the other direction only to see the thickness of the snow has thinned a bit within the woods. I can at least see the ground now, instead of a blanket of white.

"Where did you go?" I whisper to the raven. "I've lost you."

As though it has heard me, it caws from above the treetops, yet when I look up, I cannot see it. The wind kicks up, and the trees whistle feverishly. The raven caws again, this time louder. Its cry echoes through the quiet, cold forest, alerting other creatures of its presence. Flocks of birds scatter, flying off in different directions, and they begin to circle above, creating a funnel of wind. I stand up, stepping away from the ledge, frightened.

Fog rolls in with perfect timing. It's thick, and I can't see anything in front of me. This isn't good at all. One wrong move and I'll tumble to my death. My heart beats fiercely, and I'm frozen in fear. Fear of moving away from the funnel and fear of falling down the ravine. Either way, I'm dead where I stand. I feel the force of strong winds push me backward toward the gorge. I drop the glowing stone at my feet and grab a nearby tree branch, hoping it will hold my weight. I use my other hand to protect my face. Peeking between my fingers, I catch a glimpse of two glowing blue dots through the whirlwind. It distracts me for a few seconds. The incoming gusts go unexpectedly calm, shutting off instantly, leaving the forest placid. Like I've entered the eye of a storm, except instead of a clear day, fog remains. I have this feeling I'm being watched. I look down noticing the stone that led me here no longer glows, and I pick it up.

"Have you come to claim your calling, my child?" a voice says, behind me.

8

THE INVISIBLE BRIDGE

THE WOMAN IS AS I remembered, even after five years. Her grey hair still shows a hint of black streaks, leaving the impression that she once had lush dark hair. Her eyes are crystal blue, complimenting her strands. It's ironic to see her appearing old because her skin is smooth, absent of any wrinkles.

She holds in her hand a knotty staff that has seen better days. Perched upon the top, the same raven I saw in the woods with luminous blue eyes stares at me and then caws.

"I would agree, Krackle," she replies. A grey hooded cloak veils her body, covering a white linen robe underneath, that has a braided cord wrapped around her waist with light blue tassels hanging down about her ankles.

"It's really you." The stone in my hand glows again, but this time it's bright green.

She turns around, walking away. "Follow me if you wish to know the answers you seek." In a hushed voice, she says, "Tell them we're on our way." The raven she calls Krackle flies off.

I put the glowing stone back in my pocket and follow behind her down a narrow path. "Where are we going?"

"You'll see." The woman is slow when she walks, making it easier to keep up, unlike the raven flying in the sky, that is until the fog thickens.

"Wait," I say, as I try to keep up. "I can barely see in front of me." The haze is so heavy the woman fades in and out of view.

She stops. "It will be all right. The lower clouds help to camouflage our way. Do not veer off the cobblestone path, though, else you may fall to the canyon below."

"What cobblestone—" I look down to see grey stones beneath my feet— "path." Stunned by what I see, I add, "How did I not notice them before?"

The woman chuckles and continues forward. "Because they were not there before. As long as the mist is present, the cobblestones will remain. I will explain later. Time is not on our side. We need to press forward before the fog fades."

I consider my options to go our separate ways, but something influences me to keep following despite what my gut says.

A few minutes pass, and we come to the end of the trail. A massive boulder stands in our way. "What now?" To our right lies the drop-off to the gorge below, and to our left, there are tree roots, soil, and rock. This trail feels like we're following along the side of an overhanging slope. "It's a dead end."

She turns around and smiles. Her eyes sparkle with mystery. "Is it?" She doesn't appear worried. "This way," she says, stepping off the cliff.

My heart sinks, but I'm quickly relieved to see she doesn't fall to her death as she hovers in the air.

The woman looks down at her feet. "I assure you, I'm still on solid ground." Underneath her feet is the same cobblestone path we've been traveling on. She appears to stand on air, but when she stomps, the cobblestone reveals itself briefly, then fades. She chuckles. "Not something you expected, I gather?"

I huff. "Having faith isn't one of my strong suits." I look at her with doubt, knowing that I just saw with my own eyes a solid cobblestone a second ago beneath her feet.

The woman laughs. "You still don't believe me? Will this help?" She stomps her foot, again. The sole of her shoes clank against the invisible surface. Again, the stones appear and then quickly fade. "Like I said, you're safe. It's solid. I assure you, Petra, you won't fall."

Shock jerks my head up. "You know my name?"

"Of course, I do."

I raise a brow and take in a deep breath. "Right, because I'm the granddaughter to the King of the Underworld."

"I suppose that's one way of looking at it," she agrees.

"But?"

"You're much more than an heir to the throne. I see a great future ahead for you."

"What do you mean by that?" Curiosity has me sewn into her message. I can't pull away from her words. I take a step closer, not realizing I've stepped off the trail until I look down. I shriek. "What exactly is this trickery?"

"Not a trick, more of an illusion. It's an invisible bridge," she says. "Follow close, the path is narrow. Be sure to step where I step. There is about one foot on either side of you, so be sure to focus where I walk, or you'll drop to your death."

"That's comforting," I say under my breath.

"Trust me, you don't want to cross this overpass once the fog clears. We've wasted much time already, I'm afraid we may need to make a run for it." She glances up, and I look with her. "The sun will burn off these lower clouds soon." She turns. "If it makes you feel more comfortable, grab onto the back of my cloak." The woman continues across, confident in each step she takes. "The answers to your questions are waiting on the other side of the valley."

Trusting what she says, I take a faithful step, squeezing my eyes shut. But I quickly find my feet landing on solid stone as the woman predicted, and I look to see the cobblestones appear under my feet. My mind is in awe. "I've never seen such sorcery."

"It isn't sorcery, my dear. It's magic. This bridge was built by the Fae. It mustn't kiss the sun to cross."

I try not to allow the fear to take hold and follow where the woman steps. "We better move quicker," she says, hobbling faster to reach the other side. "No more hesitation, Petra, we need to cross now."

The afternoon sun begins to burn off the mist, and I feel it start to warm. The fog is thinning, and I gaze up to see a glimmer of light showing through. Some of the cobblestones disappear where the glare shines upon them, while some cobblestones crumble, breaking away and fall to the ravine below, as the rays of sunshine hit the path.

"We need to make a run for it," she says. I see a glimmer of sunlight beam down in front of us. The woman leaps over the gaping hole where the light shines on the pathway. "Petra, hurry up!"

Her panic spurs me on and I jump, too. One of the stones breaks away from my heel, nearly making me fall. The woman makes it across, urging me to run faster. A few more stones break away ahead, forcing me to get a running start. I jump again, making one giant leap, landing on solid grass, and fall to my knees, out of breath.

"We made it across just in time," she says.

I sit up as both of us witness the bridge slowly crumble away as the sun shines brightly upon each cobblestone that the light hits. The thundering sounds of rocks falling against the valley walls echo, leaving me in awe.

My heart returns to a normal beat, and I put my head between my knees breathing in deep to calm my nerves. "That's the most intense thing I've ever been through."

The woman clucks her tongue. "That's nothing compared to some of the things ahead."

"What do you mean by that?" I ask.

She smiles. "You'll see. Come, we're almost to the gate."

9

THE LIQUID PORTAL

THE LANDSCAPE ON THE other side of the gorge is different, with fragrances riding through the breeze from the colorful array of flowers dotting the grass, unlike the wintry scene where we came from.

"Quite the contrast," I say, looking across the cavern to the dreary forest that hides under the blanket of crystal snow.

The woman comes by my side. "A stark reminder of how different our seasons can be."

The snow covers the fir trees and icicles cascade over the ledge but here, the balmy sun beams upon my shoulders, warming my frozen body. "It's so magical," I say. "I mean, I've gone from the dead of winter to the birth of spring in a matter of minutes."

The trees and foliage on this side brims with life. Thick grass carpets the ground and colorful trees sprout from the soil. Birds sing and leaves whisper across the warm gentle wind. It makes me think a life of peace is possible. It has me feeling a bit freer from the dread of being discovered. Looking back across the vast valley, it's like night and day.

I point. "All we did is cross that invisible bridge. I don't understand how we're a short distance away, yet the side we came from is winter, but where we stand it's the beginning of spring."

"And if you were to stand over there now, all you would see here was the same. On that side, we too, appear icy and cold."

"You mean there's an illusion that it's winter here, too?"

"This might be hard for you to understand, but I'll try and explain best as I can. If one decided to cross now, say fly because it's impossible to walk across, all they would see and experience is more of the same—snow and ice."

"What if someone built a bridge?"

"What if they did?" the woman smiles confidently. "No one can pass to our realm where the Fae thrive."

Meeting Sylvie comes to mind. Did she know all along that this was the way to seek the old woman? I keep that thought to myself for now.

The woman looks into my eyes. "You would be wise to stay in good faith with Fae folk, my dear."

I nod.

The woman smiles. "Wait until you see Wisteria Keep." The same cobblestone path begins lighting the way and we follow. "It's a place where magic is protected, and those who wish to escape oppression to seek a peaceful life, live. It's also the only gate leading to Ladorielle."

"I've heard of this sister planet. My mother says it's a dangerous place."

The woman laughs. "Compared to where we are now, one would call it paradise. I suppose for dark witches, vampires, necromancers, or even werewolves, they would call it dangerous to live on Ladorielle, too, but for those with good intentions, it's a much better place than here."

I follow alongside her through the enchanted woods with its lustrous beauty, realizing her words hit close to home. Deep in my soul, I don't want to be the grand-daughter of the King of the Underworld. "Why do I have the feeling you understand me?"

"Because I do. More than you know."

I watch fireflies buzz around, reminding me of earlier when I discovered they were really Fae. They don't light up during the day, but I can feel them sweep by every now and then. "You're not going to tell me more about Ladorielle, are you?"

"Maybe in time, when you're ready."

The silence between us becomes a little awkward. "Can you at least tell me about why the bridge is invisible?"

"It's different, isn't it? You must be vetted before crossing the invisible bridge."

"How so?"

"Remember Sylvie?" the woman asks.

I smile. "I knew it. She's the reason I found you, isn't she?" This makes me wonder how much she knows about me. I stare past her to the knotted woods ahead. "So, who are you?"

She huffs as if I should know and smiles. "My dear," she says softly, "do you not remember?"

"No, no not really. I remember coming to you when I was a little girl, and you gave me this." I pull out the stone from my pocket.

"And a valuable stone it is, my child. I knew we would someday meet again."

"Are you the Eye of the Raven?"

The woman smiles. "What makes you ask that?"

"Sylvie."

The woman gives a soft grunt. "Is that so?"

She hesitates to say more.

"I've heard the stories. You're a legend."

She chuckles. "So, you've heard of me, eh?"

Her words bring me chills. "A seer that calls to the past, present, and future? Yeah, I would say the world knows who you are. You're like a big name around here. Some call you The Raven."

"Oh, I wouldn't go that far. An old woman like me can't get around like I used to."

I swallow hard. "I'm presuming you know mine... the future, that is?"

She smiles. "Many forms of it, yes."

"I don't follow."

We come to a fork in the road. "Free will, dear." She looks at me. "Shall we go left, or right?"

I scowl. "I don't understand. Are you not leading the way?"

"This is your path, not mine. I'm here to guide you. Here's your first test. Which path is the right one?"

"I don't know. Why do I have to choose? Why can't you choose for me?"

"Because it isn't my destiny."

When I don't make a choice quick enough, she adds, "You will have many more difficult decisions in the future. What does your gut say?"

"I—I don't know." I turn left, then right. Both paths look identical. Then I turn straight ahead. "Neither path."

The woman smiles.

I step forward, off the cobblestone trail, and when I do, what was once a dead-end forms into a third path. I laugh.

"I do believe you're getting the hang of it," she says.

"Okay, please explain. You said I wasn't to veer off the cobblestones."

"And yet here you did it anyway." She creases her brows.

I look at her, frustrated.

She takes in a deep breath. "When you took that first leap of faith, at the invisible bridge, knowing there was a deep cavern ready to swallow you up whole, you followed your instincts instead, allowing your mind to open up to the possibilities."

"Are you saying that was free will?"

"It was a choice, wasn't it?"

I stew a bit on her comment. "And I did it again just now?"

"Precisely."

"But will it lead us to the same destination?"

"Of course." She grunts. "So many questions. Haven't you heard that too many of them can get one in a bind?"

"Sorry."

The woman stops. She points as she turns to me, saying, "And that's another thing—never apologize for wanting to learn. Asking questions is a good thing."

I nod, taking in her advice. "My mind can't comprehend all of the possible outcomes of the future and thinking about it gives me a headache."

"In time you will begin to understand." She starts walking again. "Now, where was I? Ah, yes, free will. You see, everyone has a choice. We make decisions based on that choice. That determines my visions. So, they can change quite frequently."

"Sounds very complicated." I hesitate to press her again with my unanswered questions but decide to carry on. "So, do you have a name—I mean other than me calling you, Eye of the Raven?"

"Mmm, yes, I do suppose that might be easier on us both," she says. She walks a few more feet, as though deciding on whether to answer me. "You know, no one knows I'm the Eye of the Raven except you. My identity is somewhat secret." She sighs.

"What do you mean by that?"

"I'm sure you have heard of rumors." She smiles.

Suddenly, I don't feel as comfortable with this woman as before. I can sense something isn't quite right.

"I suppose you're going to have to know sooner or later." As we walk, I see her struggle to keep pace.

"Are you okay?"

"I'll be fine. I'm just tired." We walk up a small hill as she continues the tale of her past. "Before I became the Eye of the Raven, people called me Thermyah." She huffs. "They still know me as her. I've just changed a bit is all."

I'm about to ask why when I feel a warm vibration come from my pocket. I pull out the stone and watch the lustrous gem brighten. "Why is it doing that? I've already found you."

"Because we're near the portal that leads to Wisteria Keep."

The closer we walk to the portal gate, the brighter the stone becomes.

The Fae buzz by us by the thousands once more, like they did when they lifted me to the blue hollow oak tree, but this time they look like glitter reflecting off the sunlight.

"You can tell we're near the city gate when we see these lovely creatures flying about. They're the guardians of the gated entrance."

I squint, wondering how something so tiny can be a guardian.

"Never underestimate a small individual, my dear. That would be a mistake. For you see, the smaller creatures have an advantage. They've come to expect that, and when that happens, you will lose."

All the glittering Fae collectively form into a large glowing ball of light.

"Here we are," Thermyah says.

Confused, I look around and I see nothing but trees all around us. "What do you mean?"

Krackle appears from the sky and swoops down, landing on Thermyah's shoulder and greets us with a caw.

"Yes, we made it safe and sound," she answers and stamps her staff on the ground. Out of nowhere, an oval circle appears in the center of the bright light the Fae made.

"What is that? It looks like water." Inside the shape is a shimmering liquid with an array of colors in purples, pinks, and blues.

"It's the portal to Wisteria Keep."

The oval portal isn't too large, but it is big enough for a human to fit through.

"Go ahead, stick your hand through it."

I hesitate to follow her instructions, but intrigue has captured my soul, and I place my index finger through the liquid. It feels cool, slightly numbing my fingertips. I push the rest of my hand in slowly. The sensation flows through me like swimming in water. Stunned from its loveliness, I pull back and discover my hand is dry. "How is this possible?"

The woman chuckles again. "It's going to be fun teaching you the discovery of magic." She lifts her chin, nodding for me to pass through. "Go on, I'll be right behind you. Quickly now, I'm losing energy." I watch her face become strained.

This could be a trap; however, if she wanted to kill me, she's had ample opportunity. I step through the liquid portal, and what I see on the other side takes my breath away.

10

WISTERIA KEEP

IT'S AS THOUGH I'VE stepped into a different world. Almost similar to when we passed the invisible bridge. The colors are the most vivid that I've ever seen, with bright fuchsia, deep purples, vibrant yellows, and oranges. I feel magical energies kiss my skin and it soothes my soul, relieving any worries I previously had. My body feels healed, too. No longer do my legs ache from walking, and my hunger pangs have disappeared. Although I'm famished, it's bearable. "This is an amazing feeling."

"You might also feel your mind at peace, too," Thermyah says, closing her eyes with her face to the sky.

She's right. The fear and dread are gone. "I do," I say, smiling. "How about you?"

"I can feel my energy slowly returning, yes," she says. I see Thermyah's features transform. She's youthful now, looking maybe a few years older than me. Her salt and pepper hair now flows in an ebony sheet, with white stripes threading the front, and the raven that is her familiar changes to a man before my eyes.

I'm startled by both their transformations.

"How is this possible?" A breeze catches my hair in the wind and strands tickle my nose. The fragrance of jasmine invades my senses, along with the whispers of lighthearted voices that stir beyond the protected gates. The distraction tugs at me.

"You're at the base of Wisteria Keep. It's the highway to both our worlds, Ladorielle and Elleirodal."

"I get that, but I'm still wondering how you managed to become young." I look at Krackle. "And you, you're a shifter."

"A raven shifter to be exact." He puts out his hand. "I can't be in this form outside the realms of Wisteria Keep."

"Interesting." Looking back to Thermyah, I say, "I understand what you mean by more is yet to be discovered." I focus on Krackle. "It must tear at you to not be able to walk the lands beyond this kingdom."

"It's the curse of my bloodline, I'm afraid." He eyes Thermyah as though he knows not to say too much.

She smiles. "Shall we go inside?" Thermyah asks. Clearly, she is trying to distract me from asking more questions. I tuck that thought away for now.

"You two go on, I need to take care of a few things. I'll meet you back home," Krackle says. He rushes away, as though late for an appointment.

"Is Krackle his real name?"

Thermyah chuckles. "No, of course not. His real name is Kraig."

The trellis entryway is made of wisteria branches that cross over, making an arch, with lavender and purple flowers dangling. Cypress trees line the perimeter as a fence, bordering the legendary fortress.

"You know, Thermyah, I've heard of such a place as this. Most people think of this realm as a myth."

"What do your eyes see?" She puts her hand out gesturing us to move forward.

"A magical place that is indescribable."

The thoughts of my mother come into focus. She will stop at nothing if she finds out this place really exists. The rest of my grandfather's kingdom isn't on board to listen to such nonsense, but if my mother convinces them... I take in a deep breath, thinking about the chaos my mother might cause. "If she finds me—"

"We have taken all precautions, I assure you. Not to worry," Thermyah says. "I'll take you on a small tour, but first we need to eat. Are you hungry?"

"Starving, actually."

The gates automatically open as if expecting us, and I feel a surge of power pass through me. "What was that?"

"Faeland energy," Thermyah answers. "It's how the kingdom protects against dark magic should something ever get past the guardians of the gate."

As we step across the threshold to the city hidden behind the trees, two guardsmen stand post on either side of us, observing our every move. A cobblestone path, much like the same one that led us here, veers off in many directions.

I gasp at the sight of so many people; Fae, fairy, elves, dwarves, humans... "Vampires?" I look at Thermyah, stunned. Their flawless skin is a dead giveaway. I've been wrong a few times by misjudging on appearance alone, but for the most part, vampires are a beautiful species. They use that beauty as their weapon to lure their victims into submission.

She grunts, as if not wanting to admit it. "Some, yes."

"But they're murderers. They kill for blood." I stare at the man dressed in fine clothes. His blue eyes are striking. A rush of panic flows through my veins. Can he hear my thoughts, my heartbeat? His hair is ice white and tousled. He sports a square jawline and a dimpled chin. His tunic is tightly wrapped around his body, showing off the rippling muscle hiding beneath. I can tell he isn't any ordinary vampire—he's a warrior.

Thermyah nudges my shoulder, breaking our connection. "Avoid eye contact."

"Wait, he can see me? But I'm still wearing this cloak."

"Well, that proves he has good intentions." Thermyah stops. "Invisible cloak? Wait a minute. Take that cape off a second. I want to see something."

"Why, what's wrong?" I ask, handing her my cloak.

I watch as she inspects the garment and finally pulls from the pocket the care instructions and reads. She smiles. "But of course. It's all starting to make sense, now."

"What is?"

"Your cloak doesn't hold up against the Fae Folk. Which is why I didn't realize until now that you're not invisible to me." Thermyah squints. "Tell me how you happened upon this garment?"

"It was a gift from my uncle."

Thermyah gives me a dubious glare. "Impossible."

"I don't understand. Why are you staring at me like that?"

"Because I know the person who makes these coverings."

I gasp. "That must mean my uncle knew the tailor. He probably knew about Wisteria Keep, too."

"Knew?"

"Yes, he died fighting for what he believed in. My father's brother Artan."

Thermyah raises a brow and appears to be a bit suspicious of my information.

Unsure whether to continue, I add, "He gifted it for my birthday."

"I see." We keep walking as she speaks. "Tell me more, please. I'm interested in knowing more about your discovery."

"Well," I go on, "I just recently discovered its magical abilities. If not for it—" I point to the cloak— "I would have never escaped the underworld palace." It's then I clue in, something doesn't seem to add up. Why is she asking me these questions? Isn't she a seer, after all? "How is it that you're able to see me while wearing the invisible cloak? I mean I thought you knew."

A fireball ignites, startling us. A jester blows flames from his mouth, doing tricks, and onlookers clap, cheering for more.

She hands the cloak back to me. "I think we will pay a visit to the tailor that made this, but first we eat."

But she's a seer. Shouldn't she have known?

We walk through the crowds in the center courtyard where the entertainers continue to perform stunts. They distract me, too.

"The people here look different, I know. And I'm betting you're wondering how so many species can harmonize in the same place, but I'm sure you have figured out most are Fae."

I notice Thermyah keeps her head forward, avoiding eye contact with bystanders.

She continues, "Some you will find are not of the human variety and most are of the magical kind."

"I don't think I've seen so many Fae in all my life," I say. I mean, they look human, yes, but there is a slight difference. While their ears are pointed somewhat, it's not blatantly noticeable by any means. Their hands are slimmer, their figures lean, but all their other features look human. "How do they hide their wings?" I ask softly.

"They're tucked underneath their skin."

"How strange."

"Different perhaps than what you're used to seeing, I'm sure. But as I said earlier, this place is the highway to the other world."

"It begs the question, though, if this place is so secretive, how did my uncle manage to give me this cloak?"

Thermyah stays silent. It's almost as if she's in a daydream.

"Thermyah?"

"Hmm?" Her lost expression has me confused.

"This cloak made me invisible to my family and the entire kingdom. How is it that the Fae, or you, for that matter—" I stop as shock flows through me. "Even the vampire back there saw me..."

Thermyah chuckles. "That man you saw isn't any vampire. And I assure you, he was looking at me."

"You?"

Her slithering tone tries to avoid a truthful answer. "He's expecting a package. He can't see you because you're wearing the Cloak of Invisibility."

"So, there is a name for it?"

"Quite the obvious name, I suppose," she adds. "And also, quite expensive. Honestly, until a few moments ago, I had no idea you were wearing such a precious gift."

"But you're a seer."

"You're correct. I still have flaws like any other soul. Besides, the cloak doesn't need to emit protective magic unless it senses danger. And despite the assumptions, seers cannot tell the future like a psychic. We must hold an item in our possession to manifest our visions."

"I don't follow."

"What I mean to say is I don't suddenly see the future, I must cast a spell first, or hold an item for me to see. As for that cloak, it was designed to ward off evil intentions. It will sense them, thus hiding you from view."

I gape at her confessions.

Thermyah grins. "Don't look so stunned. That's nothing compared to what you will discover living among the Fae Folk."

"And here I thought the invisible bridge was amazing."

"Come, let me introduce you to some fabulous food. The meals are to die for."

"Not literally I hope."

Thermyah smiles. "No, of course not. That would be the restaurant down the road."

I gasp.

"I'm teasing." She nods, pointing with her eyes to a café along the main path from the center courtyard. "Mosstoad Grill and Café."

"That's a restaurant?" I ask. It has a cabin-like feel. Hanging green moss grows along the ridge, with mushrooms growing atop the roof. Outside people laugh and chatter at tables that are strategically placed along the wraparound porch, with not a care in the world that the building looks like it will collapse at any moment. "It looks like a shack."

"Appearances can be deceiving," she says. She stops before we make our way up the front steps. "Perhaps it would be wise to put the cloak in your bag for now. Those that live within my city that are not Fae might find it odd that I'm talking to myself during lunch."

I snicker at the visual. "That might be rather entertaining," I tease.

Thermyah gives me a stern glare. Clearly, she isn't amused.

"Okay, fine," I say, and I unclasp the collar. Gently, I roll the garment rather than folding it, and place it in my pack.

"This is one of the most unique restaurants you may ever encounter." She pulls at the entrance doors and we walk inside.

11

SOMEONE FAMILIAR

S EVERAL PEOPLE LOUNGE AROUND the entrance, as
we pass the threshold. Many sit along the walls waiting
to be seated. "It's so crowded."

"We might have better luck downstairs." Thermyah proceeds to the wide central staircase. Carved marble statues
are set on either side of the stairwell, from floor to ceiling,
acting as pillars. I draw closer noticing they look like a king
and queen.

"They are the reigning king and queen of Wisteria
Keep," Thermyah says.

"Interesting." As we descend to the lower level the voices become louder. A stage is set up in the far-left corner of the space. In the center of the room is the bar. "It's so..."

"Busy?" Thermyah finishes. "Yes, and in the evening the local bands play. Quite the nightlife scene."

We're stopped just a few feet from the stairs, where a hostess stands, taking names. "Are you sure we want to wait? Maybe there is someplace else less crowded?" I ask.

"It's lunchtime. It will be packed everywhere we go. Besides, by the time we get to the next place, we probably would've been seated here, if we were a little patient."

Agreeing, I take in the enormous atmosphere.

"I gather you've never been outside your castle grounds, have you?"

"We have restaurants in our kingdom, of course, but not of this magnitude. This place is quite staggering."

"Wisteria Keep is an enormous city. Close to a billion population, I would venture to guess."

"Wow, that large?"

"Not something you expected?"

I shake my head as we wait in line to add our name to the waiting list.

"Haven't you been to another city?" Thermyah asks.

Again, I shake my head. "Only to the beach, camping, or hunting. My family didn't like me leaving the grounds of the fortress."

"Hunting?"

"What? Don't be so shocked. I know how to hunt." What I don't say out loud is my father was the one doing the dirty work. I just observed. "To be honest, I've never killed a living creature in all my life."

"I thought so." Thermyah walks up to the hostess at the front podium. "Two please."

The girl looks at me curiously, and I see a glint of red in her eyes. Her hair is long and black, matching her uniform. High cheekbones accentuate her heart-shaped face. The hostess puts on a fake smile, saying, "It will be about twenty minutes." She's holding back how she really feels. I can tell by her glare. She notices me staring and smiles, showing a hint of her extended fangs. She's a vampire, I'm sure of it.

Thermyah nods. "Fine."

"Name please?"

Thermyah grins and says, as she looks at me, "Petra."

I observe the girl jot down my name.

Thermyah pulls at my arm, and we sit down on a cushioned bench, waiting for our table.

"Why my name?"

Thermyah raises a brow, giving me the answer.

"Right, the 'name' thing." I feel uncomfortable asking, but I do anyway. "Why don't you want anyone to know your name?"

She doesn't answer.

I take the clue and change the subject. I point to the bar where I see many people drinking and being obnoxiously loud. "We have a few pubs where I come from. Father says I'm never to go inside them."

She grunts. "I forget you've led such a sheltered life. "Do you know what ale is?" she asks.

"Of course, Father drinks it all the time, and after several of them, he keels over until the morning."

She laughs.

"It's not funny. Sometimes people who drink Father's ale end up getting the center court members into brawls."

"I'm not chuckling because it's funny, my dear. It's because you are so naïve of the ways of the world."

"I'm not as naïve as you may think, Ther—" She nudges my arm. I point ahead of us. "What are those square things with pictures on the walls? I've never seen such magic like that before."

"You mean the televisions? In this city, you will find an eclectic array of things, people, items, cultures...." She crosses her arms, smiling. "This city is the travel hub to other worlds, dimensions, galaxies, and realms. We gather information from other places and create it for our liking here on Elleirodal."

"You mean there are other living beings in places other than our sister planets?"

She chuckles again and whispers in my ear, "Even time travel."

I gasp.

The hostess interrupts. "Your seating is ready."

We follow close behind as she leads us to our table, and I observe families with children eating in booths while in the bar area, burly men sit on stools, shouting at the screen on the wall. The only woman in the bar is the bartender. I don't understand why folks are mesmerized by what Thermyah says is television. More shouts roar, causing me to shrug my shoulders inward.

"The favorable team just made a home run."

"A what?"

We make our way to a table near the kitchen.

The hostess hands us our menus. "Your server will be with you soon."

"Thank you," Thermyah says. When the hostess leaves, she adds, "A game called baseball. It's a human game. Picked up from a galaxy rather far from here, and not easy to travel."

Stunned, I say, "Right, you did say something about time travel. I'm still trying to wrap my head around that one."

"You will experience it soon enough, but first we eat."

I pick up my menu and can't read any of it. Thermyah gives me a patient smile. "Don't worry, I can order for the both of us."

A loud burst of laughter comes from the bar, drawing my attention. I watch the back of a man's head as he talks with others. His voice sounds familiar, but I can't seem to place it.

"Is everything all right?" Thermyah asks.

I take in a deep breath, turning back to her. "It's nothing, I thought I saw someone I knew. But that would be impossible." I look back over at the bar, and the man is gone.

A server greets our table, disrupting my focus. "I'm sorry it took so long." She dips into her pocket for a pen, saying, "What can I get you two?" Her dark hair and scaly skin reminds me of the Iknes Shaw. Snake people. Many of them hang out along the pass between my grandfather's kingdom and the adjacent one to the west. *Edmond's castle.* Fear stirs within me, knowing his father is going to be angry. They too will probably join forces in search of me.

I look over at Thermyah, knowing I haven't a clue what this restaurant serves.

"Two Moggle Pops, please," Thermyah replies. "We still need a few minutes."

The girl nods and starts to go, when Thermyah adds, "Oh and ah, Spike Dip."

"Of course," she says.

Thermyah smiles. Her face looks delighted, as if anticipating my thoughts on the dish.

I tilt my head, dubiously. "As in the same deadly Sea Spike urchins that scale the ocean floors?"

"That would be them."

"I—I'm not sure—"

"Don't worry, silly, the poison evaporates once the meat is cooked. It's delicious."

"Interesting. I didn't know it was edible."

The server quickly returns with our drinks. "Two Moggle Pops," she says and sets them next to us. "Your appetizer will be on the way. Are you ready to order?"

Thermyah glances at me. "Do you like fish?"

I shrug. "Sure."

Thermyah hands the menus to the girl, saying, "Two Blackened Salmons, please."

"Good choice. It happens to be the special of the day, too."

"Great," Thermyah says.

"So, this is a Moggle Pop?" I sip my drink. "Taste just like lemonade, but with a tart kick."

"It's quite the hit here."

The server returns quickly with the appetizer, and after she leaves, Thermyah pushes over a bowl of chips, that accompanied the dip. "Try it with this."

85

When I don't budge, she chuckles. "Ok, I'll go first then, will that help?" She scoops her helping and practically inhales the food.

"Guess I'm not the only one hungry." I smile.

Thermyah huffs. "I didn't have breakfast."

I raise a brow. "You know that's not healthy."

"Neither is my profession." She takes a second helping of dip. "Might want to dig in before I eat it all myself."

I decide to take a chance. I mean, she's already had ample time to kill me, right? I plate a serving and take a tiny stab. "It tastes like an ordinary seafood dip but spicy."

Thermyah chuckles. She takes another scoop and pops it into her mouth. "It's my favorite dish."

Soon our table is served with the main course, and there is so much of it that I can't finish.

Thermyah asks for the check and as were waiting, two men approach our table wearing silver chest mail. I notice the filigree emblem is the same as the symbol I saw on the trunk of the blue oak tree set at Hollow Forest's edge. I feel the stone warm hiding inside my pants pocket. *Something is wrong.*

One of the guards comes down by Thermyah's ear. I can't make out what he says.

She pierces a glare. "Are you sure?"

"I wouldn't be here, madame, if it wasn't serious."

Thermyah's mood changes, sending a glare my way. "It's time we go." She places money on the table. "Petra, my dear, we must pay a visit to an old friend."

"Is everything okay?"

"Fine, fine." Thermyah's coy tone doesn't slither past me. She's hiding something and doesn't plan to share.

"Let's scoot," she says, not waiting for my response, and quickly walks toward the back exit.

Once outside, I ask, "What was that all about?" I'm annoyed by her abrupt exit.

"There is so much more to do," Thermyah says, ignoring the question. Her walk is quick-paced, making it difficult to keep up.

She isn't going to tell me, and it stirs a little distrust within. "Is this about my mother?"

She still doesn't answer. Her brisk walking has me concerned. The streets bustle with people, and I begin to lose sight of her. Frustrated, I shout, "Thermyah."

She stops, as do the rest of the people in our vicinity. Strangers stare, with a few of them approaching me. I shouldn't have said her name out loud, and I begin to feel tightness in the pit of my stomach, too.

A middle-aged woman carrying a basket of goods, asks, "You know Thermyah?" Coming up close to my face, she inspects me up and down. "You're not from around here, are you?"

I take a step backward. "I-I—"

Another stranger tugs at my elbow. "Where is she?" His amber eyes pierce through me as though he's attempting to invade my thoughts.

"Get away from me." I pull out of his mindful grasp. "There must be some mistake." I take a couple more steps backward. There are so many people that soon, I'm surrounded.

If only I had the cloak on. I gasp. *The cloak, that's it.* I quickly pull it out of my bag and drape it around my shoulders, but it doesn't work. The townspeople still hound me with questions, and pull at my arms, and some try to make eye contact, to invade my thoughts. *Why isn't the magic working?*

12

EYES AS BLUE AS MINE

"THAT'S ENOUGH!" I HEAR a stranger call out. "Let the girl be."

"But you heard her," one woman argues. "She's seen Thermyah."

"The girl merely called out her name, it doesn't mean she's seen her face." The stranger pushes through the crowd. "It's all a misunderstanding, I'm sure, isn't that, right?" he asks, staring deeply into my eyes.

I quickly recognize him as the same man who took my breath away with his blue eyes and striking white hair, in the courtyard earlier near the entrance gates to Wisteria Keep. "It's you."

He smiles. "Me?"

I smile back. *Do not make eye contact.* I sever our connection and look down. *I'm wearing my cloak. He, and the rest of these folks can see me. I'm so confused.* "I—I'm sorry I thought you were someone else," I lie.

He rumbles a low grunt. "Folks, there's nothing to be alarmed about. Please, all of you, go about your day." He puts out his hand, still staring deep into my eyes, adding, "Perhaps I can be of some assistance?"

He's not a necromancer like me, but his irises are as blue as mine. His gaze is mesmerizing, and forgetting my better judgment to pull away, I take his hand. "Sure."

The crowd dissipates and we find ourselves standing alone along the cobblestone walkway.

"I'm Bryce," he says, bowing. "And you must be Petra."

I freeze hearing his words. "How do you know my name?

Pleased by my reactions, he goes on to whisper, "I think I know where *she* might be."

"You know—" I stop and look around, making sure no one is in earshot. "You know…Thermyah?"

He laughs. "She's my mother."

Raising a brow, I say, "Your mother?"

"I can explain more, but not out here in the open." He changes the subject. "Where were you headed, anyway, before you shooed her off?"

"I don't know. Ther—" I swallow, trying hard to hold down my food. "This is all so upsetting. I'm sorry, I'm confused, and I have so many questions."

He nods. "That's understandable." We casually walk along the sidewalk as he continues, "Perhaps we should go to her home to see if she's there?"

"I guess that's a start."

I look to the opposite road and see a boy no older than ten selling newspapers, while people of all shapes and sizes walk by. What strikes me the most is many of the Fae Folk don't fly. "I clearly don't understand. I mean if I had a choice between walking and flying, why that's –"

A man crosses the street a little way in front of us. It's the same person I saw at the restaurant.

Bryce notices. "Someone you know?"

"I'm not sure." Distracted, I step onto the street without looking. A horn blasts, grabbing my attention and I feel a hand pull me back.

Stunned, I watch an odd contraption on four wheels fade in the distance. "What is that?"

"A transport coach. You know, you should be more careful before stepping into the road. In the Earth's universe, they call them cars."

Sidetracked by what I see, as the driver slowly glides out of view, I ask, "What's a transport coach?"

He chuckles. "You haven't been out much, have you?"

I huff. "Funny, your mother said the same thing to me earlier."

I look across the street. Logic creeps in. After experiencing how hard it was to get to Wisteria Keep, I doubt the man in the bar is the person I'm thinking of. Irritated by the close call to death, I say, "No. I've never been outside the fortress of House of Zhir." I stiffen, straightening my clothes. "We don't have such contraptions in our kingdom."

"And there it is. The truth comes out." His sharp tone bites.

I squint in annoyance. "What's that supposed to mean?"

"It all makes sense now. When I heard my mother's name, a name not to be spoken out loud for any reason, I knew it had to be you. I hadn't believed she would pull it off, but seeing you now, with my own eyes, I understand why."

"Care to share?"

He gives an irritated rumble. "My mother is beyond passionate about certain things." His square jaw flexes as though he's retaining to say how he really feels. "She was determined to find you. Hearing you say that wretched kingdom does bring everything into focus, though."

His agitated pitch sends me nervous vibes. He's gorgeous, but beneath his façade is something mysterious and dangerous. I can feel it. A soul I'm not sure I can trust yet. Although he did just pull me from the brink of death. "Ah, I see... you're making a judgment out of pure assumptions. I'm my mother's daughter, is that it?" His undertone manners coils beneath my skin. I don't like where this conversation is headed. "You knew who I was before you met me a moment ago."

"Yes, well, my mother didn't say she was bringing the Princess of Zhir to our doorstep. Just that your name was Petra and that you would be coming to live with us."

"Us?"

He huffs. "Yes, I still live with my mother." He stops to reflect. "Well, in the apartment next to her, so not exactly in her home."

"I would imagine a man your age would want to cut the apron strings."

His features turn a shade of red. "Don't be so alarmed." He simpers, curving a coy smile. Ignoring my stinging tongue, he adds, "Perhaps we should look there, first."

"Your home, or hers?" I bounce back. Clearly, he plays me for a fool. I'm not a timid schoolgirl.

"It's not far, trust me."

"And why would I go to a stranger's home I just met not five minutes ago?"

"That's fair." He tilts his head, bowing. His cool smile and piercing gaze tell me, he's much more than Thermyah's son.

He is harboring a secret of his own. "Wait here, and I shall fetch her myself."

He dashes out of sight before I have time to protest.

13

CHANGES

A LONE ON THE STREET corner, I begin to feel a little uncomfortable, yet not afraid. I still have the cloak about my shoulders but wearing it has posed to be contradictory. Sitting down on a nearby bench, I pull out my journal and begin writing down the events. Maybe it will give me some insight as to how to deal with all my emotions from today. Ironically, I don't feel afraid of being in a strange city unaccompanied. Quite the opposite, actually. For the first time, I feel freedom and it feels glorious. No one next to me to tell me where to go, or what to do. This would be my moment, right here, right now, to seek the portal gate to Ladorielle.

The thought of that adventure quickly fades when footsteps approach and stop. Recognizing the robe and light blue tassels dangling about the persons ankles, I look up.

"I'm sorry for abandoning you."

I huff. "I don't understand any of this. And I don't like being kept in the dark," I say.

"I know." Thermyah holds out her hand. "I'll take you to my place where we can talk more freely."

Taking in a deep sigh, I place my journal back in my pack and stand, saying, "Okay."

WE WALK ALONG THE cobblestone walkway leading to the center of the courtyard where people advertise their wares, attempting to lure customers to buy their goods. Vendors line the edges of the path.

A merchant cries out, "Get your pastries here, and you don't have to eat for a week."

I put a hand over my mouth, whispering, "A week? I've never heard of such a thing."

"Neither have I," Thermyah replies, chuckling.

I pause in thought thinking back to meeting Bryce, and I say, "So you have a son?"

"I do." She looks sad when confessing the truth.

"Why didn't you tell me?"

"I wanted to tell you at the right time."

"But when we entered through the gates, you had your chance then."

"Too crowded. And I'm not about to bear my dirty laundry out for all to see."

Dirty laundry?

She grunts. "Let's just say the past is not something I talk about in public." She glances over her shoulder. "Save the questions until we're behind closed doors."

I raise a brow and cross my arms.

"Please?" she asks.

I nod, changing the subject, and ask something a bit less private. "Do Ladorielle people come here? I can't imagine anyone wanting to live near the warzone of our world right now."

"Some do, yes. Vacationing, perhaps, but to live? No, you're right about that. Why would anyone want to live on Elleiro-dal where chaos is everywhere you turn?" Thermyah glances around. "The Fae have managed to keep this area hidden for a while now, but I fear our time will run out soon if things don't change quickly."

Tilting her head, she looks at me with concern. "For example, you. It's only a matter of time before your mother will come looking."

"Is that why we left the restaurant in such a hurry?" I can tell she doesn't want to talk about that subject.

After careful thought, she answers, "Someone else is here in the city, and not your family. They're looking for me."

"Really? Wow, a bounty on the famous Eye of the Raven," I murmur. "Imagine that." I smirk.

Thermyah sneers. "Yes, well, this hunter isn't like any you may have seen."

We keep walking down the center strip of town. A few people turn, noticing us, making me feel a little uncomfortable. Thermyah, notices, too. "We should head to my home where we can discuss your questions further."

As we walk down the path toward Thermyah's home, she says, "Sometimes I forget that most outsiders don't read the language of the Fae. Once we get you out of those clothes and cleaned up, you will fit in like everyone else."

A flock of birds are spooked from the nearby treetops. Thermyah grabs my arm. "Hold on, we're getting out of here."

Before I have a chance to question her, she reaches for my palm and stamps her staff to the ground. In seconds we've leaped to a different section of the city.

I'm in awe. "That isn't something I expected."

"We're still within the walls of Wisteria Keep but slightly outside the village. Now, we're away from prying eyes."

"You think we're being followed?"

"Well, you did bring attention by saying my name out loud earlier."

"I'm truly sorry about that. I knew it was a mistake, seconds after I said the words."

She nods. "I understand, and I know you have many questions. My home is just a few more steps."

In the far distance, I see a giant tree I didn't see from town because of all the buildings and hills. I point. "What is that? It looks like a massive—"

"The tree?" the old woman interrupts. "It's the gateway to other worlds."

Reminded by Thermyah's fear, of people knowing her identity I say, "You know, I watched Grandfather bind *her* powers."

"Your mother's?" Thermyah asks.

I nod. "With the snap of his fingers."

"Well, I'm sure he'll give them back now, knowing you've disappeared. Her magic is powerful. It will take a delicate balance shielding you while still performing the ritual tomorrow at midnight."

I stop. "What ritual?"

Thermyah attempts to soothe my worries. "Petra, you turn eighteen in one more day. Tomorrow, you must choose a side before the strike of midnight. If you do not, your soul will be forever captured in time, sending you to Scarlet Hollow."

I tilt my head. "What's Scarlet Hollow?"

Thermyah's brow creases. "Your parents never told you?"

I shake my head.

"It's a realm where the banished go, the souls of the dead walk the surface, and the supernatural live. It's what the folks in the land of the living call the In Between."

"Purgatory."

"Similar, yes."

The thought of living in eternal hell doesn't sit well. "You don't have to worry about me. I've chosen a side already."

She grins. "Oh, I know that. It was as clear to me then, five years ago, as it is now. However, I feel you aren't sure of the choice you've made."

"I'm unsure of the future. Besides, I wouldn't be here in Wisteria Keep if I hadn't made my choice already, am I right?"

"Yes and no. You're still seventeen. There's still time for you to change your mind. I'm here to help you make the right choice. And so, we need to perform the light witch ceremony before your birthday to protect you. It's the same ritual your parents would perform had you stayed, the only difference—" Thermyah stops and stares at me. "Well, would you look at that?"

"What?" I turn behind me, thinking she's looking over my shoulder.

She chuckles. "There's no one behind you, silly, it's your hair."

"What about my hair?" I grab a few long locks and see the dark, shiny ebony strands turn a stark white. "What's happening?"

"It's what happens when a witch born with dark blood chooses to do light witch magic. This is proof you have already chosen. I do admit I was a bit worried earlier this afternoon before stepping onto the invisible bridge. Your hair should have changed then."

"So, you can look at my hair and know?"

"This doesn't happen to everyone. Only dark witches that have chosen to do light magic, or that of dragon bloodline, and well since dragon shifters are extinct, we know you're not that. Many witches have been able to hide their color by dying it."

I eye the white strands in front of Thermyah's face. "Like yours?"

"I wasn't born a dark witch. My white streaks come from my father's side."

I think back to when Uncle Artan showed a few tufts of white in his hair. "People go grey all the time," I point out.

"Indeed," Thermyah agrees.

"So how can you say this?"

"Unlike people going grey over time, the transformation of the white hair only happens to a young witch before they turn eighteen."

"And what if someone chooses to change their ways after they turn eighteen?" I've heard gossip of this happening once to a nobleman of the court.

"They will always have a dark side, my dear, lying dormant. Those people are the ones capable of unique powers. They learn to balance but can still be easily influenced should they hang out with the wrong crowd. These people make good hunters." She stops and turns. "Of which you are not." She smiles again, and we continue on. "We need a few things before the ritual, but that can wait until tomorrow. Tonight, we rest, and you will study your part in the ceremony."

"My parents have prepared me my whole life for this moment but became frustrated recently because none of the lessons they were teaching me would work. I've never been able to deal magic."

"There will be plenty of time for that in the future. The good news is a light witch can always practice after they turn eighteen, whereas a dark witch cannot."

"That must be why my mother was determined to unbind my powers last night. I overheard her telling my father, accusing you of binding them."

A triumphant smile curves her cheek. "I don't regret doing it either."

"Does that mean you will unbind them?"

"Of course, I will. What's a witch without her powers, my child?"

We continue to walk along until we come to a fork in the road and veer to the left. The pathway ends with a tree standing in the middle. A small door snuggles in the trunk. "And here we are." Thermyah takes a key and unlocks her door.

14

A TREE HOUSE

W HEN WE WALK INSIDE, I see stairs spiral upward.

"Many of the Fae folk live among the trees," Thermyah says as she begins to ascend.

I follow.

When we reach the top, we're high above in the trees. We walk outside onto a huge deck that connects to several suspension bridges. Each catwalk joins to another tree. "It's like a tree house town," I say. "I've never seen anything like it." The tree we're in gives a view of the city.

"We have one more flight to go," Thermyah says.

"We can go higher?"

"Come on, I'll show you." We spiral upward as I take in the spectacular views. "Wait until you see it at night. It's quite serene."

We reach her place. A door is framed out in the trunk like the one we entered from downstairs. "This is my home." She opens the apartment, and we walk inside.

"This is one spectacular structure, Thermyah. I've never seen anything quite so unique before."

She places her keys in a bowl sitting on a stand next to the front door, saying, "This particular tree has three apartments. The one across the way—" she points – "has two." She grins. "My apartment isn't even the top tier."

"It's definitely exceptional, I'll give you that." The place is cozy and cute but a bit on the small side. A wood stove sits in one corner, and next to it is a sliding glass door leading out to the deck, featuring amazing views of the city. "It's beautiful up here."

The afternoon sunlight seeps through the thick branches. "It's getting close to evening. It'll be dark soon," Thermyah says. "We have so much to prepare for." I watch as she grabs cups from the cupboard and prepares a kettle of water.

"Drinking tea is the first step in your journey of awakening."

"Tea?"

"Right, I forget you are not familiar with the process," she says, as she turns on the burner. "This is the same method as if drinking blood for the dark ritual."

"Ew, gross." The memory of my mother taking blood samples from my sisters and herself comes to mind. "I've seen the ritual before. I know how it works. It comes with a human sacrifice as well." Humans are the one species who don't have magical powers.

"There will be no human sacrifice tonight," Thermyah says. "I assure you of that." She pops off the lid that holds the teabags. "Do you prefer black tea or green?"

"Either is fine, thank you."

Thermyah smiles. I see her choose the green. "This one will help us focus more."

Her small kitchen resides at the opposite end of the fireplace, with more spiral stairs adjacent to the kitchen, leading up to a second level above.

I look up and see a bed in the loft. "Quaint," I say.

"Small but it works for me." She puts on a kettle of water. "Now, shall we get you out of those wretched clothes and into something more suitable?"

I look down at my body and realize she's right—I am in quite a disarray.

She points. "My room is upstairs, as well as a bathroom where you can bathe. There's a second-level loft up there, too. The stairs are behind my bedframe. Quite the illusion, I admit. You won't see them until you come around the bed. The guest room is small but hopefully, you will find it an adequate place to sleep for the night."

"Thank you. I'm grateful for your hospitality."

Thermyah smiles. "It's no trouble, I promise."

I haul my heavy bag up the stairs and quickly settle in the guest room. Thermyah was right, it is small. More like closet size. No wonder she uses the bedroom below. There is only enough space for a single bed, nightstand, and dresser. A small round window above the bedframe lets in a tiny bit of daylight.

I quickly change out of my clothes and run a warm bath. I'm looking forward to the escape of loveliness.

Just as I'm about to slip into the tub, a knock on the door startles me. "Petra, I hope you don't mind. I brought your tea and set it on the nightstand in your room. Drinking tea while I take a bath has always soothed my nerves. I hope it helps."

"Thank you," I say. *Soothes my nerves?* I wonder if she senses my feelings.

B Y THE TIME I get out of the tub, the tea has cooled to almost lukewarm. Still wrapped in a towel I take a sip. The taste of mint, blackberry, and cinnamon, swirls in my mouth as I swallow. It tastes wonderful. I take another sip quickly. The sensation of pure joy flows through me, as though all my worries have left my mind, and I sit on the bed capturing the moment. It's a moment of peace I don't think I've ever experienced before, and it feels amazing.

Noticing that the sun has hidden behind the trees outside, I realize it will be dark soon. Setting my empty cup down, I hang my cloak up on a hook behind my bedroom door. I'm sure we're here for the rest of the evening.

I change into something more comfortable and put on black leather bottoms, and a matching top that blends well with the cloak my uncle gave me. I'm loving the pockets the cloak hides, too. There, I place the stone Thermyah gave me all those years ago, as well as my small journal. I also tuck my pack under the bed to save room, and then grab my empty teacup and head back downstairs.

It isn't until I look over the edge of the upper loft outside my room that I realize it's a three-story drop. From here I can also see amazing views of the city. That would probably explain the two chairs seated next to the railing.

I look down to the bottom floor of Thermyah's apartment, quickly become queasy, and sit. I hear her doing dishes below. Catching a few deep breaths I descend the stairs to the living area, taking in the unique character of the space, and proceed to take a seat at the kitchen table.

"Feel better?" Thermyah asks, sitting across from me.

I nod, handing her my empty teacup. "The bath was lovely, and the tea was a perfect remedy."

"Would you like another?"

"Yes please, thank you."

She adds a second bag and removes the first, then pours the hot water, saying, "I figured we should begin by talking about what to expect between now and tomorrow."

I cup my hands around the warm beverage and breathe in the steam. "Sounds great to me." She's right, I haven't a clue how light witches do their rituals. It would be nice for her to explain it.

"We need to gather a few things to prepare for tomorrow night. What concerns me, however, is your hair." She raises a brow and nods for me to turn around.

A large mirror stands against the wall. I walk over and peer at my reflection, stunned. "I've never seen anything quite like this." I finger-comb the strands. "How is this possible? I mean I figured a few white streaks sure when you warned me my hair would change, maybe the salt-and-pepper look like you, but my whole head?" I turn around and stare at her. "My hair has gone completely white." I turn back around, staring at myself in awe. "I mean in a matter of minutes. Upstairs it was still black with only a few white streaks. I even had a plan to strategically hide the white, but this... this will be impossible to conceal."

"Don't worry," Thermyah replies. She comes around her small kitchen island to comfort me.

"Don't worry?" I ask, still shocked by what I see.

"I have a wig. It will hide the hair, at least until we can change the color. I agree that a girl your age having white hair will draw attention. Tomorrow while we're in town, we'll get some hair dye."

"I look like I'm twenty years older." I want to cry. "Is this my punishment because I won't choose to be dark like my family?"

Thermyah wraps her hand around my shoulders. "Come sit with me. Let me explain."

We sit down on the sofa, and Thermyah hands me a tissue. "You still look beautiful."

I wipe my nose. "Thank you."

"When a witch from a dark bloodline chooses light, changes begin, and one of those changes is hair color."

"Guess that explains why I never saw this before." I look down at my hands, half expecting them to whither and wrinkle. "Dark witches must wait until the phase of a blood moon to capture their dark power. And must savor it until the next blood moon." I look up at Thermyah. "What happens to born light witches?"

"Their hair doesn't change if that's what you're asking."

"What does change?"

"They draw power from the elements. They begin to feel differently."

"And the dark witches that decide to choose light, like me?"

"The same will be for you, too."

"And if they're almost eighteen like me and decide to choose dark instead of light?"

Thermyah studies me. "Why are you asking such questions?"

I sigh. "Because I had a dream. More like a vision. I saw a girl my age born of light, and right before her eighteenth birthday the dark had called her, and she took in the demon. It possessed her. I don't want that for me."

Thermyah is silent for a good stretch before she answers. "When a born light witch chooses the dark, she becomes a possession of the underworld. Her body might look like a light witch, but her soul is not. Very few can see through their façade." She grabs my hands, cupping them. "I'm more concerned that you saw this vision. Have you seen many in the past?"

I nod.

Worry etches Thermyah's face.

"Is something wrong?"

"Not at all." She lies. I can see right through her. She's hiding something she doesn't want to tell me.

I swallow, not sure if I should press the issue. I don't want to make her irritated. I'm in her home, and she's been kind enough to take me in. I change the subject. "You mentioned the passageway to Ladorielle earlier. Can you tell me more?"

"I can, yes, but first you must learn how to deal with the aftereffects of your changing spirit. If you're not prepared, it could be deadly for you."

"Deadly?" Her words cut deep. Am I doing the right thing? Running away at the time seemed like the logical solution. I recall the evil intentions of my mother and father. The words they said before I made my escape. Anything is better than the life I had before.

"Are you ready to proceed?"

"Not exactly, but you must know something, or you would have never brought me here." I hesitate to say more. "My mother—"

"Yes, I know all about your mother and her intentions."

"You do?"

She walks over to the kitchen island, grabs the kettle and condiments, and set them on a silver tray. "You will be ready by tomorrow at midnight. I have no doubt of that."

I sigh. "My mother never told me in detail what's supposed to happen. Only that my powers as a necromancer will exemplify. I don't want to be like *her*."

"I know." She pauses as though what she's about to say will be painful for me to process. "Listen, I want to tell you something..." She walks to the living room and sets the tray down on the coffee table. "Come sit with me on the sofa."

I grab my mug and follow.

"I was a Fae before I became the Eye of the Raven. Had wings and lived here in the village. A story for another time I suppose but I was lucky enough to continue living here among the Fae Folk. The people here don't know I'm the Eye of the Raven. Nobody does..." She hands me a biscuit. "Except you."

"Why are you telling me this?"

She smiles. "I'm a seer, remember?"

"But you said the future changes. Are you saying my visions are of the future?"

"Possibly. I don't know, only you can determine that. But from what I gather, you're not about to go back to the life you once had, am I right?"

I shake my head. "Not a chance. I've made my decision. I will not carry out the evil ways of my mother's line. I want to leave this area and never come back. That's why I asked you about Ladorielle. I've seen things a child should never see, Thermyah." I dip my scone in my tea and take a bite.

"Then there are a few things you must know before we can proceed."

"Like what?"

"Well, for starters, why do you want to leave Elleirodal? You can thrive here in Wisteria Keep, as many others do. Elleirodal is a large planet with billions of beings living in cities all over the world."

"This land is evil, or have you not noticed the demons my grandfather hires?"

"I've noticed, but there is also good. Is that not true of Wisteria Keep?"

"Sure, I suppose. But it's only a matter of time before that will change."

"Ah, so you have seen what I see." Thermyah grunts a soft laugh.

"I don't need to *see* to witness the catastrophes my grandfather and mother have in place for the future."

Thermyah sips her tea. "I cannot tell you of my past unless you accept its responsibility in knowing the truth."

"I don't understand."

"I know you don't, which is why I have someone you must meet first." She sets her cup down. "The first step in the ritual is to meet Fate."

I nearly choke on my tea. "Come again?"

"Magic has a cost, and you must see what kind of cost it will bring. Fate has a purpose. Magical witches make choices daily—you are no exception. It is important for you to understand that each time you use magic, it alters the path of the future."

"Wait, so you're saying Fate is an entity?"

"More or less." She nods, indicating I should turn around.

Appearing before my eyes is a shadow. Soon, it forms into a person in a black robe. "Petra, meet Fate."

I stand. "This isn't possible."

"Why?" She grunts. "Keep an open mind. He's here to show a future."

"But I thought you did that, with being a seer and all?"

"Ah, but the difference between mine and his... Fate's foretelling will not change. As with all the seers before me, we all had a visit with Fate before proceeding with the ritual. A necessary step."

It suddenly begins to make sense. "Wait, are you saying I'm a future seer?"

"That's my assessment, yes. You did confess you saw a future of a girl yet to be born." She smiles, as though she, too, saw the same.

Fate doesn't speak, only puts out his hand for me to take. "Go on, Petra, it's time you know what the future holds for you." Thermyah stands, grabs my hand, then her staff, and stamps it on the floor. Immediately we're transported to another space and time.

15

A DATE WITH FATE

S TEPPING INTO A DIFFERENT world with Thermyah is a little unexpected. Fate points, drawing my attention to the center square.

"This looks familiar," I say.

"It should. It is Wisteria Keep," Thermyah says.

The church in the center square has burned to ashes, and only the massive bell remains. A few flames flicker underneath it. My stomach churns, and I can't help but think I know who did this. "My mother."

Thermyah tilts her head, as though she agrees.

"She's angry with me for fleeing her world, her wrath, isn't she?"

"You're assuming this is the future. What if this is the past?"

"Because I would know if it was."

"Is that so?" She looks at Fate, as though to be awarded permission to say more.

"There is no other who can make such destruction. My grandfather, yes, but he would never stoop to this level. I mean, killing innocents like this? It's insane. It isn't his way." I look at Thermyah, and pain is written on her face. "Are you saying this is a past event?"

She shrugs.

My eyes fill with tears. "I'm no match for her, am I?"

"A match for her? Petra, you're already above her morals, you've pushed her from your life and already made a statement by running away to better your own. The question is, where will you go from here?"

"Thermyah, look at this city. It's destroyed."

We're interrupted by a girl walking in the center of town. Her clothes are scorched and her face is dirty. She doesn't appear injured, but she clearly has seen better days. She isn't crying, but her face undoubtedly shows anger and fear.

The smell of hot coals and burning flesh consumes my senses. "Please, can we go back?"

"Not yet," Thermyah says.

The hissing of molten embers sings revenge in my ears, and I feel what this girl is feeling. I don't know how or why, but I feel the fury boiling inside her. The connection is so strong I feel my body become her. I know her thoughts, past, present, and future. I gasp, realizing the truth, as I stare back at Thermyah.

Above me, I hear the cawing of a murder of crows among the treetops. One comes down and lands by my feet. Except he's a raven. Larger, tougher, and smarter than the flock that trails behind him. He looks exactly like Kraig. His mate, Meeka, lies lifeless on the ground. I kneel. "I'm so sorry," I say. I have no control of my body. I'm stuck inside the vessel of this young girl, experiencing her emotions, saying words she says.

The dead bird transforms into a woman. I'm shocked by what I see, but the girl I'm possessing says, "You tried to warn me. To tell me this would happen, but I didn't listen. This is all my fault." She begins to cry, lying over the dead woman's body. "What can I do?" A tear falls from my eyes, landing on the chest of the woman, soaking her clothes. The body crumbles underneath me, leaving a white haze in its place. The wind picks up, creating a funnel, much like it did when Thermyah first revealed herself in the frozen Hollow Forest. The dead woman that once lay on the ground now appears before me as a spirit. "Do you accept your fate now?"

I cry, but it's not my tears I shed, but the girl I possess. "I do, please come back."

"I cannot, but I can leave with you my magic. But it comes at a price."

"Anything. I'll do anything."

"You must take my place. Until you fulfill your debt."

I nod. "Agreed."

She looks at the Raven perched on a nearby plank, which forces me to see once more the devastation. "So much death."

"Yes," Meeka says. "But I believe you will make it right."

She disappears, leaving me alone. The raven caws and flies off. "Where are you going?"

I follow him through the town. I'm not sure there are any survivors. The anger begins to build, and I feel a new sense of strength soar within me. A surge of power flows through my veins. My wings might be gone, but there is still hope flowing through me. I will seek my revenge until every last soul is freed from bondage.

They haven't seen the last of me... They want evil? I'll show them the definition of evil. Yes, I understand that in war there are casualties, that loved ones die for what they believe in, but this? I look around at the devastation... this is insane. "My sister is dead." Still possessing the girl, I feel the tears well in my eyes just thinking about the possibilities of other people perishing. I run to my folk's house. "No!" I cry. I can see the vision. I see the past as clearly as I see what is in front of me. My home lies in ashes. I reach the hill where our cottage once stood, confirming my vision. "Please," I pray, "please tell me my parents escaped with their lives."

I look up to the sky, screaming, "Tomorrow is another day. Tomorrow will be the day of reckoning, and those daring to cross my path, may the skies above have mercy on their souls. For the underworld may have won the battle this day, but I will win the war. May the energies of my ancestors flow through my veins for I have found the true meaning of my gifts. This is the day I lose sight of all that is good or evil. I will seek justice!"

The painful memories reach my soul. I fight the tears as my familiar caws, perched upon my shoulder. My eighteenth birthday flits across my mind. I remember waking in chaos and ruin, with my fist still closed. I opened my hand to see the Hawk's Eye seared my palm and transformed into a tattoo, leaving behind my gift. It was too small to be a dragon's egg, although why would I receive something like that anyway? I'm not a light witch—only they can acquire such familiars. Usually, when a dark witch such as me turns eighteen, it's a bird of some sort. I'm no different. Occasionally, a witch will receive a unique familiar such as a cat, bear, or wolf. But like the house of Shadow Raven and the sisters before me, I received a raven's egg. This familiar would be my companion for life. Dawn awakens the lands with shining shades of oranges, reds, and yellows upon the uncovered graves of men, women, and children. As I stand here on the castle floor, I think about how I will seek my revenge. This fight brought great evil here today, and the Fae people suffered at the hands of Vothule.

I look back to watch Thermyah and Fate observing me. "This is your past, not mine. Why did you show me this? Why did you push my soul into your vessel?" The pain is so raw, so real, it's like Thermyah and I are now forever connected.

The raven finds me and lands by my feet, transforming into a man. The same man I saw at the portal gate. "Krackle?"

16

BOOK OF SECRETS

THE SOUND OF RAINDROPS wake me, and I realize I'm in my room tucked underneath warm covers. Feeling a little disoriented, I sit up and look around to see nothing is out of place. The empty teacup still sits on the nightstand and my cloak hangs on the back of the door.

"That was the weirdest dream I've ever had," I whisper. The house is quiet, and I almost think I'm alone when I hear snoring from below. I pull off the covers and realize I'm still wrapped in a towel. I must have fallen asleep after my bath.

Wait a minute. I try to think of my last moments. It's so foggy. I must have been more tired than I thought. Feeling a slight deja'vu, I dress in black bottoms and matching top. Instead of going back downstairs, I open my backpack and pull out the large book I took from my grandfather's drawer. I hadn't had the chance to see the pages inside.

The top of the cover has four clear crystals in each corner, with a linear line drawing to the center of the book. There, one large blue oval stone attaches in the middle where all four lines meet. It takes a few seconds before I realize this is the same design of the symbol on the blue hollow tree trunk. On the front of the cover in swirling letters it spells *The Book of Secrets.*

I go to turn the first page when I hear, "I wouldn't do that if I were you."

Startled, I drop the book and turn. "I—I'm sorry, I didn't hear you come up."

It isn't Thermyah standing in my room, but Kraig.

"I didn't mean to disturb you." He puts out his hand, as though to stop me. "Please, don't open that book."

"Why? What do you know about it?"

"It's actually a portal. If you open it, you run the risk of being shipped to another dimension."

My eyes widen. "Are you serious?" I look down at the cover. "I briefly opened it before in my grandfather's office."

"Impossible," Kraig argues. "The only way to successfully open that book without being teleported to somewhere else is if you sprinkle Fae dust upon it. The dust will disrupt the book's power preventing it from casting magic."

I think back to when I saw Tharin sprinkle what I assumed was glitter in his hands. I raise a brow, making the connection. "I don't think we have anything to worry about," I say. I flip the cover open.

"No!" He leaps to grab the book, but I'm quicker, tucking it under my arm. "Wait a minute." He looks around, turning a full circle. We're still here." He squints, confused. "How come we're still here?"

I'm beginning to realize the importance of this book. "What exactly is this *Book of Secrets* anyway?"

Sitting at the end of the bed, he says, "It's a time travel book. It can take you to the past, present, or future. You cannot open the book on your own, less you want to find yourself in another place not of your choosing. The book must be allowed to choose for you."

"Kraig?" Thermyah calls from below.

"We're up here," he says.

"It's so weird to see you in human form and not as a bird."

"No one here in the city knows except our son, and now you."

Thermyah reaches the top of the stairs.

"Right, I remember meeting Bryce earlier."

Kraig looks over at Thermyah, confused. "When was this?"

"Yesterday." Thermyah eases up the last step.

"Yesterday?" I ask. This confirms that I was so tired after taking a bath, I fell asleep.

Kraig looks at her in surprise.

"She would have found out sooner or later," she says.

Kraig seems annoyed. He doesn't say a word.

Thermyah looks over at me, noticing the book. "What have you got there?"

I bite my lip, not sure what to say. Kraig nods for me to go on.

I hand the book to her. "Apparently, it's *The Book of Secrets*?"

She takes it. "Interesting. Where did you find this? We have been in search of it for centuries. Ever since the destruction of Nevis' Lazoria. It was taken from the portal hub, inevitably destroying the planet."

"But I thought it was because of our dying sun?"

"My dear Petra, this book was the sun's core. It's the book that held the entire magical universe together. Whoever stole this book is responsible for the destruction of our sun."

"And the reason the planet of Nevis' Lazoria sacrificed its magic to save the rest of us," I say.

"So, you know the story?"

"Not all of it, no."

"We need to get this back in the hands of the Nevis' Lazoria people," she says. She glances at Kraig. "We should take this to Annabelle. Maybe she can figure out a solution to keep this book safe."

He nods. "Before we go, I have one quick question: how did you know that the pages were dormant?"

I take a deep breath. How am I going to explain this without going into detail? "I watched someone sprinkle magical dust over it. He was caught attempting to steal it."

"So, you stole it instead. Clever girl," Kraig says.

I observe both Kraig and Thermyah stare at each other, communicating in silence. "It seems we're not the only ones who are after this book," she says.

"I better go warn the Elders," Kraig says.

"Elders?"

"The keepers of the gates. The guardians that protect this city and the only portal to Ladorielle," he answers.

"We should consider getting you new clothes too," Thermyah says after Kraig leaves. "I know just the person to help us."

I look down at my choice of outfits. "What's wrong with my clothes?"

"Nothing, but you do need to dress appropriately. You don't blend in with black leather trousers. People around here will assume you're a warrior."

I huff. "Is that a bad thing?"

"Not at all."

I gather everything I own, including my cloak, hanging on the back of the door, and quickly stuff everything in my bag. I don't trust leaving my things. Not yet anyway.

17

THE RING

I MEET THERMYAH DOWNSTAIRS. She grabs her keys, locks the door and we head into town. "Our first stop is Cat's Eye Corner," she says.

As we head down the spiral stairs, I say, "I had a really weird dream last night."

"I'm not surprised, you blacked out cold after your bath. I tucked you in. Can I ask what it was about?"

"My dream?" I turn to look at her, biting my bottom lip. "I was you."

Thermyah chuckles. "Well, now, that is quite the dream, isn't it?"

"No, you don't understand. You weren't the Eye of the Raven, your sister was."

Thermyah stops. Her eyes grow dark and sad. "Meeka," she murmurs.

"So, what happened?"

At first, I don't think she's going to answer, then she says, softly, "Your mother killed her."

"What? But how can you be sure?" My soul aches for her loss. "Never mind, forget I said that. She's done awful things. I've seen it."

Thermyah takes a deep breath. "It happened a long time ago. I would rather not bring up the past right now." Thermyah's solemn face shows deep regret. I don't need to push the issue. If that dream is any indication of a truthful story, I know her pain.

We walk along the cobblestone path through the city in silence until we stop at a cute stone building that looks more like a cottage. "A glitter walkway?"

"Well, you are in a town full of Fae," Thermyah replies.

"Right."

The shop is set in front of a large blue oak tree, with an adjoining wraparound porch, decked out in clear lights that twist around the gables and railings. A staircase spirals upward around the trunk with another building attached above.

"How odd," I say.

She turns and smiles. "You will find most species in this city live among the trees with the businesses residing on solid ground. I like this store in particular because it's like a one-stop shop. I bet it's a little crowded. I usually come in the early morning, like now. Shall we?"

I nod.

The door opens with a bell at the top jingling, letting the clerk inside know of our arrival.

"Welcome," I hear a voice say but don't see them. There are a few other customers inside shopping as well, like Thermyah mentioned.

The shop has music playing so it distracts me. I suddenly feel the need to dance. My head begins to shake, and my body begins to move to the rhythm of the beat.

"Oh dear," Thermyah interrupts. "We need to get you earplugs."

Before I have a chance to understand what she means, she stuffs my ears with cotton. "What was that for, I was enjoying—" My mouth falls open, realizing what I just did was completely out of character. *I don't dance.*

"The music doesn't affect anyone but necromancer witches such as yourself," Thermyah says. "You see, it's a defense mechanism built into the system. Sort of a distraction. It penetrates the eardrums, and one cannot resist its spell."

I huff. Almost annoyed. I mean, I do understand. Witches like me are trained to seek out Fae and destroy every last one of their kind, but why didn't she warn me? "Kind of risky bringing me here, don't you think?"

I get stares from other customers and a few leave, knowing what I am. "So much for hiding me."

"Yes, I suppose that is an error on my part, but people in this city must know you were inspected thoroughly before entering the community. I mean, clearly the bridge would have detected your tendencies then."

I raise a brow. My throat goes dry thinking about it. "And now my hair is white."

"That isn't as unusual as you might think. Some Fae have white hair, such as the ones that control the seasons. Spring and summer Fae have purple, pink, and yellow hair, while the autumn Faeries have brown, reds, oranges, and green."

"The winter Faeries have white, I'm guessing?"

She nods. "And blue."

She pats my shoulder. "It's nothing to worry about, really. If the invisible bridge detected any ill will on your part in the slightest as to do harm to me or any living creature, the planks would have given way, and you would not be here now talking to me."

I swallow hard. "Guess I passed."

"With flying magical colors, my dear. I had no doubt, though. I've known your heart from the first day I met you.

Not to mention you still had to get past the Faerie whisps."
Thermyah smiles.

"The guardians you mentioned before?"

"That's right. Faerie whisps—Guardians of the Gate." She smiles. "Human creatures and the like see them as fireflies."

A sales clerk comes to greet us. The woman eyes me as she speaks, "Myah, I had no idea you were here. When did you return?"

Thermyah gives a slight bow. "Last night."

"Safe trip, I hope?"

"Yes."

"Did you find what you were looking for?"

I can tell Thermyah is trying to get a word in without divulging too much. "Something like that, yes."

"Oh, that's nice—"

"Annabelle, I want you to meet my new friend, Petra."

Annabelle has young features, yet I can tell she's older than she looks. Her hair is a wavy chestnut brown, and she has beautiful auburn eyes. She's petite in stature and has flawless skin. If I didn't know any better, I'd say she, too, is a vampire, but something about her tells me I might be wrong. She doesn't look at me like I'm her next meal, and I don't see protruding fangs.

"Nice to meet you, Petra. You look to be the same age as my daughter Lily."

I hesitate to say too much, but I get a gentle nudge from Thermyah, telling me she can be trusted. "It's her birthday tomorrow, Annabelle. We've come to find supplies." Thermyah pauses, eyeing Annabelle. "Her eighteenth birthday."

"Oh." Annabelle's lips tighten. "I see. Say no more, follow me." Annabelle walks behind the counter and that's when I see a second clerk stocking the back shelf. She's a young girl not much older than me. "This is my daughter Lily."

"Hello, pleased to meet you," she says, putting out her hand. Her voice matches the one I heard when we entered the store.

"Lily," Annabelle begins, "would you please show our guest around the shop. Perhaps help her find new clothes. Myah and I need to head to the back and discuss a few things."

"As you wish, Mother." She bows at her, and this type of mannerism strikes me as strange. Is her mother royalty, too? I've seen this behavior between myself and my parents.

"Please enjoy your time here, Petra. We have many things that might intrigue you," Annabelle says, interrupting my thoughts. Dangling crystals hanging from the doorframe sway back and forth, chiming as they clash against each other, as the two women pass through them. Oddly enough, they make musical sounds as the strings swing back and forth.

I smile at Lily, feeling a little awkward. I can tell she feels the same.

"I'm guessing what they have to discuss is important," Lily says. "My mother doesn't take people in the back room very often."

Observing her fidgeting fingers, I reply, "I promise I don't bite." I try to lighten the mood, but it backfires.

Lily's feature shows suspicion. She's not amused. "I'm sorry for being forward, but are you a necromancer witch?"

Her comment catches me off guard. I clear my throat. "What a peculiar thing to ask someone you just met." I try to remain calm, as I don't think she meant anything by it. Using my intuition, I add. "Fair enough I suppose. But like Ther—"

Lily titters. "Thermyah, you can say it. We know who she is."

I tilt my head. "For someone who has told me I'm the only one who knows her name, there seems to be a lot of other people who know her name, too."

"She's, my aunt. Annabelle is Thermyah's sister."

I suck in a breath. "Oh."

"People around here call her Myah for short." I can tell she doesn't want to elaborate and leads me to an array of rings in a display case.

"Now, here we have handcrafted jewelry. Some are heirlooms while others are new." She looks at my hands. "I see you haven't any rings to decorate your fingers."

Does she know, I wonder? If she does, she's right. I don't sport a necromancer ring. I purposely left it at home. It identifies our House. "No, I suppose I don't." I look down at Lily's hand. *Aquamarine.*

She notices me staring and covers the ring quickly with her other hand. As though she understands, she says, "Forgive me, please. It's just that, well, you're the first to ever cross into our gates. I'm betting it's already all over town of your arrival."

"You're kidding, right? Is my culture that taboo that my mere presence scares everyone? I wouldn't know, as I've never come across a Fae, either."

"Oh, no... I'm not Fae, I'm a fairy mermaid."

"A fairy what?"

She giggles softly. "Mermaid. You know, we swim in the sea."

"I know what a mermaid is. I didn't think they really existed.

"My grandfather actually prefers it that way," Lily says.

My brows crease. "That you don't exist?"

"No, silly. He has an entire crew that keeps mermaids mythical. Can you imagine if word got out that we weren't a myth?"

I huff. "You can bet if my mother found out there were mermaids, she would make an entire fleet to hunt your kind down, I'm sure."

"My kind?"

"I'm sorry. Your species."

"That's fair, I guess. But you can understand why I was so forward earlier, right?"

I smirk. "So, we just met and you're telling me this because suddenly you trust me? I don't buy it."

Lily huffs. "I trust my aunt. Besides if you had any evil bone in your body, you wouldn't be here. Although I do detect a secret you carry with you."

And I'm not about to tell you, either. "I'm not who you think I am. I don't even have magical powers."

"No? I've never heard of such a thing. No magic. I mean at all?" Lily seems legitimately stunned.

My lips press together. I shake my head.

"Wow, you're like a human, then."

"Pardon?"

"Sorry, it's just that I don't think I've ever met a supernatural that didn't have some sort of magic to work with."

"I wouldn't know. I never developed the skills. My mother says an old woman bound them a week before my thirteenth birthday."

"Huh."

She pulls out a ring and places it on the glass surface. "This was found deep in the mines not far from here."

I pick up the piece, inspecting it. "No known history?" I ask. It is a dark silver ring and has a dragon carved into the metal. The head of the beast holds in its jaws a deep cobalt stone with grey swirl streaks, mimicking that of storm clouds.

"It's Lapis Lazuli. We can't seem to sell it. I've offered this ring to every customer that has shown an interest. Each time someone tries it on, they quickly take it off in a matter of seconds."

"So, you want me to try it on, is that it?" I inspect it further, taking in the detail. The dragon loops around the hollow circle, ending with its tail on the other end of the ring. Inside the rim, I read a carved signature that says, Storm. Glancing at Lily for a brief moment I decide to take a chance and slip the jewel on my right middle finger.

I feel a rush of air push me, and my veins fill with a desire for power. I have a new vision and this one isn't like the others. Before it was deep and dark, filled with death and sorrow, but this was a premonition of light, and change. *I have found you at last,* a voice whispers.

"Petra, are you okay?" I feel Lily grab my arm and walk me over to a window, where she opens it to let in fresh air.

I take a seat while trying to catch my breath. "What just happened?"

"I—I don't know. It was like you blacked out, but you were awake. I thought you were going to fall, and I rushed to catch you. Do you feel okay?"

"I think so." I look down to see I'm still wearing the ring. The stone seems brighter near the sunlight. "I'm not sure this ring is for me." I attempt to pull it off, but it doesn't budge.

Lily raises a brow. "Seems to me it's found its owner."

"But I haven't any money to pay for it."

"We will figure the cost later—" She stops. "Whoa."

I squint. "What?"

"Your eyes, they've turned ice blue."

"What?"

Lily grabs a display of hand mirrors in a basket next to us. "See for yourself."

"What's going on?"

"I don't know, but something tells me you're not who you think you are."

I nod. "Agreed. Should we tell Thermyah?"

"They're not here," Lily confesses.

"Come again?"

"They went to talk to my grandfather in the underwater kingdom."

I look over at the hanging beaded drapes, swaying from the breeze that catches them, from the opened window. "Are you saying there is a portal through there?"

Lily nods. "Way in the back yes."

"Wow, that isn't something I expected."

"I'm sure they will be back soon." Lily puts out her hand. "Come on, let's find you some new clothes. A good shopping spree will help, I'm sure. It does for me when I'm full of different emotions."

18

GIFTS AND MAGIC

A FTER A GOOD TEN minutes of sorting out my feelings and the recent events, I ask, "Forgive me for being curious... if you're a fairy mermaid, where are your wings and tail?"

She snickers. Turning her back toward me, she briefly shows a beautiful array of rainbow-colored wings that extend between her shoulder blades, then quickly tucks them back in. "I keep them hidden for the most part. I tend to get ridiculed for being different because they're not a solid color like the Fae."

"I'm sorry." I can tell this is something she struggles with. "So, what about your tail?"

"That is something I can hide more easily. I have to always take a bath because if my legs get wet, they immediately turn."

I look out the window, remembering it rained earlier. I decide not to push with further questions. Clearly, she doesn't feel comfortable talking about it.

Lily points to a line of beautiful dresses along the wall.

I tilt my head, giving a half smile. "Not really my style."

"Not in the mood for dresses?" she asks.

I shake my head. "I'm not a dress kind of gal. Actually, it makes my mother quite annoyed. Maybe something more comfortable, like slacks?" I point to the corner where I spot leather bottoms.

Stunned, Lily picks up a pair. "These? Are you sure?"

I smile. "Most definitely."

She raises a brow seeing I have almost the exact pair on, then holds them to my waist. "You know these are designed for assassins, archers, and maybe warriors, but I don't think you're any of those."

"And?" I put one hand on my hip. "You don't think I can pull it off, do you?"

"Oh, I'm sure you could, it's just that... well..." She takes a deep breath. "These trousers cater to added agility and to enhance spells when casting during combat. Will you be encountering any danger?"

"I honestly don't know."

"Well, you seem to be drawn to this style apparently." She turns and grabs black bottoms and a matching purple and black top. "How about these? They will heighten your intuition, your wisdom, and charisma." She grabs what looks like a half-circle skirt. "And this is like a cape for the bottoms. It's your shield."

"A rather interesting-looking shield," I say.

"It's not a dress, I promise."

"And what good will they do if I can't do magic?"

"Trust me, these items will help you." She hands me the garments and directs me to the changing room.

"I see a nice white sweater over there," I say, pointing to a shelf.

"Too warm," Lily answers.

"Right, I still have winter on my mind."

"Oh? Is it winter where you're from?"

"I'm from the Northern Kingdom."

"Ah that makes sense. But isn't the Northern Kingdom made up of mostly wolves?"

"Yes, but we're further west, of Crescent Keep."

Lily's eyes grow dark, as though I've told her too much. "Are you from the Kingdom of Zhir?"

I don't answer her and lower my eyes instead.

"Petra, who are you really?" she presses, focusing her aqua eyes on me. "Something tells me you're much more than just a stranger passing through. And from what I gather, Thermyah deems you as worthy, but something tells me you're going to bring danger to our community."

I clear my throat. "Lily, I honestly don't know how to answer that."

She nods, gesturing for me to try on the clothes.

After trying on the outfit Lily put together, I walk out to show her.

She curves a grin. "Yep, you pull it off well, I do admit."

I look in the mirror and discover a new me. "I swear I feel like the black sheep everywhere I go. I just want to fit in. This outfit makes me feel like I'm someone else. Like a new me. Like the *me* I'm supposed to be. I don't want to be the heir to the—"

"Stop. Don't say it. Our shop is too crowded. Petra, you can't stay here."

"Don't you think I know that?"

Lily takes in a deep breath. "Hang on, I think I might have something for you." She takes me to a large wall with several baskets filled with a plethora of different assorted gems. "We received a large shipment the other day from the Trek trader."

"Trek?" I don't like the sound of that. They're everyone's enemy. My grandfather doesn't even like dealing with them. They're a hybrid of half man, half ogre. And they can shape-shift into anything. The simple mention of them sends shivers over my skin.

"Not to worry, you will never see the likes of them inside these walls," Lily reassures. "We have a special light that the naked eye cannot see. You, yourself, passed through its rays when crossing the threshold. Had you any blood of a Trek, you would have incinerated on the spot."

"That's comforting, I guess."

"Here we are. I found it." She grabs a small stone about an inch in diameter. "This will definitely shield you from any dark magic that comes your way. I can make it into a necklace if you would like?"

I take the stone and inspect the color. It's ebony with blue stripes. "What is this?"

"It's a Hawk's Eye. The stone is rare, and we usually sell out on the first day we receive them. Our shipment came yesterday. This looks to be the last one in stock, too."

"You mean like this one?" I pull the stone looking almost identical to the one in Lily's hand out of my pocket.

She appears surprised. "Yeah. How did you get one? Not many places sell them."

"Thermyah gave it to me."

"I see."

"I'm not too familiar with what a Hawk's Eye does—can you help explain their properties?"

Lily nods. "It's commonly worn by druids."

"Druids?"

Lily smiles. "You didn't think they come this far, huh?"

"Well, I know their home is on Ladorielle. Why come here at all?"

"Hunting."

I wrinkle my nose, confused. "Like what?"

"There are minerals we have on this planet that don't exist on Ladorielle and vice versa of course. Some reside here, and we hire them to scout our perimeters for predators."

"I had no idea. Why are you telling me this?"

Lily shrugs. "Guess I like you. And well, maybe if you're lucky, you might bump into one that can port you out of here."

"Well, isn't that what the portal gate is for?"

"That gate has a long list. It will take you weeks before your name is called."

"I see. Thermyah never mentioned that."

Lily doesn't volunteer any more information, so I ask, "Do you know what this is supposed to do?" I hold the stone out for her to inspect it.

"For a druid, the stone absorbs into their skin, travels to a location on their body, and then attaches to the host, leaving a tattoo etched in their skin."

"Sounds painful."

"From what I'm told, it is; however, it also enhances their eye coordination and intuition. This will do the same for you, only all you have to do is wear it as jewelry."

"That's a relief."

"This stone will help protect you, and will give you a heightened sense of danger, should you encounter it. With practice, it might even help you with a higher sense of intuition."

"I like the sound of that." I smile. "However, I don't have any powers, remember?"

"Your birthday is at midnight, is it not?"

"How did you know that?"

"I overheard your conversation when you arrived."

She turns toward the hanging beaded entryway to the back room. "Something tells me you will have your magic back after midnight."

"You sound pretty confident."

"Honestly, I've not seen one person be denied their innate gifts on their eighteenth birthday." Lily pauses, as though she's stumbled on a revelation. "Did you know you will acquire a familiar?"

Relief settles my nerves. "Sure, I guess so. I mean sort of?"

Lily furrows her brows as though confused.

"Dark witches usually receive crows. Once in a while, a black feline, and on rare occasions a spider."

"Interesting, I knew about the crows, but not the others."

"Well, since you have no need for another Hawke's Eye, perhaps something else that might complement it. We have every type of stone, gem, and crystal imaginable," Lily says.

"I don't know much about stones or what they do." I pick up one that has an amber luster. "Tell me about this one?"

"That will take you to the future. Be careful with it. Unlike the last stone I mentioned, if you were to buy this, it would absorb into your skin and permanently make you a time traveler. And you don't have to be a druid for this one to take effect." She lifts her chin. "Usually, those seeking that stone are people on the run."

My heart pounds, knowing how close Lily is with that comment. "That sounds a little ominous."

"Our shop carries very rare gems."

"And this one?" I pick a blue stone.

"That is aquamarine. When used correctly along with that travel stone, it can take you to crystal castle, or any underwater world. But you must be wearing aquamarine to breathe underwater. Having the gem on its own won't help you. You must acquire the recipe first." She lifts her hand to show the ring she tried to hide from me earlier.

"A recipe?"

Lily points to a wall of books. "Let me show you." She goes to the shelf and pulls a tome. "Now, this book has all of the basics spells anyone needs to create a desired intention."

"But I'm not a trained witch."

"You don't have to be to perform these spells, although it does help."

I look at the shelf to see several more copies. "You have so many books. I understand why Thermyah said you were a one-stop shop."

Lily giggles. "We've been told that."

"More than I expected a shop like yours to have. I mean from the outside, your store looks so small, but clearly this is not the case." I look toward the ceiling and notice it's circular with endless spines of books.

"We're inside the tree trunk now," Lily adds. "I can show you the stairs leading upward if you want a closer look."

"No, that's okay, but it's spectacular looking."

"There's a coffee shop way up at the top called Bird's Nest Café." She reaches for another book. "Now, this would be a perfect addition to your belongings. *The Book of Insight*." She hands it to me, and I begin to flip through the pages.

"See here," she adds, pointing to the inside cover. "Once you write your name under *this book belongs to*... the book will conform to your magical talents and only you and your future bloodline will be able to read what it says."

"That's amazing," I say. "A book like this would come in handy." I quickly read through some of the basic spells and decide it might behoove me to gather a few of the rarest of the ingredients.

"Ah, I see you've found the *Book of Insight*. Excellent, Lily."

We both jump. "Aunt Myah, I didn't see you," Lily says.

"Didn't mean to startle you girls." Thermyah and Annabelle chuckle. "May I?" She puts out her hand for the book. "Petra will need this in the future." Thermyah flips through the pages. "Put this on my tab, will you, Lily?"

"Yes, ma'am." She takes the book and sets it on the counter near the cash register.

"Did you find any outfits, Petra?" Annabelle asks, flowing close behind.

"I did, thank you." I look down noticing I'm still wearing them.

"Not to worry, will just cut the tags," Annabelle says. "You can wear the clothes out of the store if you would like."

"Do you have satchels, too? I'm looking for something a bit more practical than my backpack.

"Like those?" Annabelle asks and points to a rack behind me.

"Yes, I think that would be perfect." There are assorted colors of purses, and I have a difficult time deciding.

"How about this one?" Lily asks. "I have one just like it in blue. It expands, too, so you can add more. It's called an Endless Bag."

I wrinkle my forehead. "I've never heard of such a thing."

Lily smiles. "It's also rare. But they are expensive." She eyes Thermyah.

"Add it to the list of items," Thermyah says.

"Oh no, I can't, you've already done so much," I protest.

"Nonsense. Lily is right, it's rare, but everyone should have an Endless Bag. Even you." Thermyah smiles. She hands the black bag to Lily. "Add it to my tab."

Lily nods, taking the stones and garments, and adding it to my accumulating pile on the counter.

"I'll get this all bagged up," Annabelle says.

"Petra, would you like me to make you a bracelet out of these stones?" Lily asks.

"Sure, if it's not any trouble."

"Not at all."

Thermyah and I look through the *Book of Insight* once more, searching certain recipes for last-minute ingredients we can stuff into my Endless Bag. We add them to the list of items before saying our goodbyes.

"Lily said she will have that bracelet ready by later this afternoon," Thermyah says as we leave the shop.

"You have been too kind, Thermyah. I'll find a way to repay you."

"Nonsense. It's no trouble."

I feel bad, and I'm not one to take charity. I feel humiliated, but these ladies have shown me so much kindness that it gives me hope that our world may someday find peace. I don't care if Thermyah says I don't have to pay her back, I'm going to anyway.

Magic comes with a price, but it's worth it, and I'll do whatever it takes if it means being free from the evil that is trying to plague my soul from the House of Zhir.

19

CHOOSE YOUR WEAPON

"THERE'S ANOTHER STOP WE need to make around the corner," Thermyah says. "One more item for the ritual."

"Okay." I adjust the purse I bought. It fits nicely across my shoulder, landing opposite upon my hip. "I can't thank you enough for this satchel."

"It will definitely come in handy. You could probably fit all your bags into it."

"No, really?"

Thermyah stops. "Have you never owned one? Seriously?"

I shake my head. "Never. I know I've never seen one in my kingdom before."

"I suppose it makes sense. Your kingdom doesn't do trade with the Trek."

"Is that who made these? Lily mentioned something about doing business with them for gems and minerals, but I didn't realize Wisteria Keep traded crafted items with the Trek, too."

"Yes, they reside in a small town that overlooks the canal between our continents, not far off from the Shadow Elf city."

"I've heard of these Shadow Elves. They mingle with the Trek."

"Not all of their species are bad, but they can be intimidating. We have a specific buyer that has a good rapport with the city. It's where we acquire the items to make the Endless Bags. There is a community within the city where many Shadow Elves dwell, too."

We turn the corner and walk up some steps that lead us to a lift. "This shop is high in the treetops." She pulls back the lever. "Hang onto your hat," she jokes. The lift gives a slight jerk, and moments later we're rising high into the air. "Hope you're not afraid of heights."

I shake my head. "I'm sure you would have known by now if I was."

"Fair enough." The lift stops with an abrupt halt. "Here we are." She steps off onto a wide deck, that wraps around a large tree. "This way."

I follow her around the massive trunk leading to a swinging bridge. She points. "The shop is on the other side."

I see a circular building that appears to be fixated to the trunk of another tree. "I'm beginning to understand why this city is called Wisteria Keep."

We open the front door, and immediately I feel the scent of something familiar. The shop, although dark, has the smell of fresh leather. A hint of cigar maybe, too. The walls are decorated with shoes, boots, belts, and an array of accessories.

The wood floor makes a hollow sound as we walk across it. Light music plays in the background.

"Hello, Thermyah, it's good to see you, again."

"Good morning to you, too," she says. "Is Aoes around?"

That man's voice. I know it. Thermyah walks in front of me, blocking my view. I peek around her. No one is standing by the cash register. I narrow my eyes then turn around. We're the only ones in the shop.

"Where is he?"

Thermyah points up. "On the ladder."

His back is to us. "Aoes is in the back. Let me finish hanging up these cloaks, and I'll be right down. I just finished weaving magical thread in the seams."

"Huh?" I whisper.

She pats my hand, directing her attention to the clerk. "Air drying is the most important part, Arty. No rush."

Arty? No, it can't be. I stop to observe the garments, picking up one next to me. The detailed stitching is very similar to the cloak my uncle gave me. *This must be where he bought my cloak.*

I look up at the man that still has his back to me. I can't get a clear view. His stature looks the same, but his hair isn't white, like a necromancer's should be.

Memories creep in... He made me a leather bracelet once. We were so close in age, we often hung out together as children as he was only a few months older than me. I remember he had a dream to be a tailor and make fine clothes, fine accessories, and fine wine. I laugh to myself because the wine is completely off base with the other two.

Glancing at the shoes displayed in front of me, I take notice to the stitching on the soles. It appears to be the same as his work. I remember him telling me that his stitching would be a signature someday and that if he were to ever have a shop of his own that this stitch would be in all his merchandise.

I look back at the man on the ladder and observe his posture as he hangs the newly stitched cloaks. I sneak a glance at his profile as he concentrates on the last garment.

I'm afraid to call out his name for fear he might fall by surprising him. I glance at Thermyah as she observes a glass case. She's distracted, good.

I make my way to the wall where he begins to descend from the ladder, when I hear Thermyah call, "Petra, come over here, please. Take a peek at this."

"Just a second," I say. But when I direct my attention back to the man on the ladder, he's gone.

"Did you find something you like?" Thermyah asks, looking up.

I breathe in deep. Hunting down that man that looks like my uncle will have to wait. "No, it's nothing. What would you like me to see?"

Walking over to her, I observe that it's another glass case like Lily showed in her shop, but this time it's weapons, rather than jewelry. The array of materials displayed is staggering.

Thermyah points. I look up to see another glass case upon the wall that hangs swords, staffs, mallets, and shields. "You need a weapon to protect yourself should it come to that."

I swallow back the bile creeping up my throat. "Only weapon I've ever used is a book."

"Diplomacy will only get you so far, Petra. And perhaps keeping the peace will be your future gift, but it won't protect you now."

"My whole life I've never fit in. My family is completely opposite of moral standards from me. I used to think it was the binding spell you cast upon me five years ago but looking at these weapons makes me ill, and I'm beginning to wonder if something is wrong with me."

"There's nothing wrong with you," Thermyah whispers.

Another clerk comes over, dressed in leather attire, draping a heavy linen apron. "Myah, it's so good to see you again."

She smiles, saying, "Likewise, Aoes. I would like you to meet, Petra."

"So, this is the mysterious Petra I've heard so much about."

I raise a brow, and clear my throat, not knowing what to say. I nod, instead.

Aoes is younger than I would have thought to own such an establishment. His hair is sandy brown, and he has a goatee to match. His high cheekbones and thin jawline accentuate his features. He's handsome, but something about him is mysterious. I can't put my finger on it, but he isn't what he appears to be. He has an accent too, and it isn't from anywhere local.

He shakes Thermyah's hand. "Is there anything you would like to see?"

I shake my head. "None of them, thank you."

Thermyah pats my shoulder. "She's looking for her first upgrade."

"I see, well you have come to the right place. May I have your palm please?"

"That's a strange request," I say, hesitant to give what he wishes.

He puts out his hand. "I assure you, I mean no harm. I need to know what kind of innate talents you have before we continue."

Thermyah nods. "This is how one screens those who wish to buy. You must be screened for your magic to improve."

"I thought you said this was for protection."

"That too."

Aoes presses for my hand.

Reluctantly, I give in and place my palm upright. "How do I know you won't—"

"Miss, this is how we have always done a weapons trade. I assure you, reading your palm is safe."

He takes my hand and traces the lines. "Uh huh."

I crease a brow, giving Thermyah an uncertain glance.

She ignores my worry, firming her lips, directing me to pay attention.

"Oh, this is interesting indeed." He takes out a monocle for a closer look. "Impossible." The glass drops from his eye. The man is clearly stunned by what he sees. He steals a glance at Thermyah. As though they communicate silently, Aoes clears his throat. "Yes well, you my dear, are a rare breed indeed."

"What's that supposed to mean?" My heart races.

"Do you believe me now, Aoes?"

He nods. "I do indeed."

"Believe what? What is going on?" I demand.

The man calling himself Aoes looks to Thermyah for approval. When she nods, he says, "You're the only one of your kind. I'd say it was an impossible theory, but I see your palm and read it with my own eyes. You're not who you think you are, my child." He glances back to Thermyah. "You know what will happen if anyone finds out, don't you?"

"I'm fully aware, yes. That's why we're here, Aoes."

"I'm only an apprentice. I cannot give you more than what I know."

Thermyah nods. "Understood."

Aoes takes a deep breath. "Petra, you're not a seer, a warrior, nor a hunter, or an assassin." He leans in. "You're not even a necromancer."

Stunned, I back away. "What?" A rush of emotions sweep through me. I don't wait to hear anymore, instead I run out of the shop to get some air.

Putting my head between my knees I sit on a nearby bench and try to keep from vomiting. My stomach is in knots. *Who am I?* I suppose I should be thrilled about finding this information, but it feels quite the opposite. Suddenly, I feel empty inside. Like I have no place where I belong. Nothing to cling to. The emptiness inside feels so hollow. Relief too. Sarmira isn't my real mother?

Footsteps approach and I see the boots of Thermyah stand next to me.

"You knew this whole time, didn't you?"

"I had to be sure."

I look up. My body is filled with anger and my eyes burn with resentment. "I don't understand. You knew?"

"Only speculated until now." She comes to sit next to me. "If anyone knew you existed, it would be a death sentence."

Tears well in my eyes. "Is that why you brought me here, so I would be safe?" I sneer, hearing her words. "How could you keep this from me?"

"I had to be sure first. And yes, I brought you here to be safe. But make no mistake, Sarmira will track you down. And when she does—"

"I don't want to think about it." I tilt my head. "So, who am I?"

"I will not tell you out here in the open. Not until I know we are safe from prying eyes, and ears."

I smirk. "Of course you would say that."

"Listen, you need to choose your firsthand weapon. It's your combat hand. It needs to be filled."

I nod. "Okay, fine. But I want answers before we start this ritual."

"I can promise you will get them by then."

We walk back inside the store where Aoes remains standing behind the counter. The back of the store is clear of anyone else. "Where is the other clerk?" I ask.

"I've sent him on his lunchbreak," Aoes says.

"Please, Myah, flip the sign behind you to close and lock the door. We don't want to take any chances."

She nods.

"Now," Aoes continues, "shall we find you some protection?"

I don't answer him.

Aoes takes from a bottom drawer that isn't out for display, several items, such as books, cards, and stone tablets. "What is all this?" I ask, confused.

"Your power isn't with combat, your power is with magic itself." He puts his palms together. "The reason you haven't any magic is because you're an elemental mage. It's time to choose your weapon."

"A what?"

He looks down at the array of items. "Choose first and I'll be able to tell you more."

"Nothing speaks to me."

"You sure?"

I huff. "Yes, I'm sure."

He glances to Thermyah.

She tilts her head and smiles. "It can't hurt, Aoes."

He pulls out a tan and brown oval rock. The daylight catches flecks of crystals embedded in the stone. It's different from most geodes, and he needs two hands to pick it up. It's of medium size, large enough to hold with one hand, yet still tiny enough to tuck away in a pocket.

"That's one impressive mineral," I say. The raw quartz begins to glow, and I feel drawn to its power. It's warm to the touch, but not hot.

Aoes raises a brow. "This is indeed intriguing."

"May I?"

He nods.

I pick up the large rock, thinking it's heavy but for me it's so light that I barely feel myself holding it. "What is this stone really?"

Both Thermyah and Aoes shake their head. "Whatever it is, it's chosen, you," she says.

Satisfied, Aoes puts away the other items and locks the case. "I'll ring you up over here."

"Wait a minute. That's it?" I ask. I want to know more about this mysterious geode.

He chuckles. "It's safer if we take care of the matter now." Tapping the cash register he adds the total. "I shall be over later this evening Myah and we can begin the ceremony in private." He hands me the geode. "Put this in your bag."

I squint, beginning to hate the position I'm being put in. "How am I supposed to trust any of you if you continue to keep me in the dark?"

The rattling at the front entrance, prompts my question to go unanswered, fuming my mind more. I've always been patient. More than most. Some people mischaracterize me as being shy, but I'm far from being that. No, there isn't a shy bone in my body. I'm observant and I take my time assessing my next move, but I'm at my tipping point. I want answers.

Aoes finishes our purchase and rushes to the door to let the patron inside.

"So sorry," I hear Aoes mumble.

"Is everything all right? It's not like you to close shop so early."

I perk up. He's back.

"Was it because of the customers that were here before I went to lunch," he adds. The man walks forward, with his familiar face staring back at me.

"Petra, is that really you?"

20

BACK FROM THE DEAD

I GULP. "YOU'RE ALIVE." All my suspicions are now con-
firmed. I don't know whether to cry, scream, or hug him,
for leaving. I cross my arms, glaring. "You're supposed to be
dead."

"You two know each other?" Thermyah asks from behind
me, sounding surprised.

Artan gives a sheepish grin, and I see his face turn red. "I can
explain."

I click my tongue. "I'm all ears, Uncle."

"Your uncle? Perhaps we should take this in the back storeroom where it's a bit more private." Clearly, she didn't see this
coming.

Artan shifts his footing, nervously. "I'll close shop."

"No need, Artan. I can do that," Aoes says. He nods to Thermyah, "I won't be far behind. Give me about twenty minutes to count down the register."

"Very well." We begin to follow her to the back when something prompts her to stop.

"Is there something else, Thermyah?" Aoes asks.

"Yes, have you seen Bryce?"

"He's down by the docks. We have a shipment coming in," Aoes confesses. "He should be back any moment, though."

Thermyah nods.

Artan and I follow Thermyah to the back storeroom. It's dark, making it nearly impossible for me to see.

"I'll get the light," Artan says, reaching for the switch.

In the center of the room is a round table and off to the side a small counter and cabinet. Several shelves butt up against an adjacent wall with boxes filled with the overflow of merchandise.

Artan pulls a chair for Thermyah.

She frowns. "I don't take too kindly to liars," she says under her breath.

Uncle Artan recoils. "No one has lied, ma'am, I assure you." He pulls a second chair for me. "Please, let me explain."

"First, I would like to know how you're still alive?" I ask.

Artan nods. "That's fair." He takes a seat opposite of us. "Remember that day your father called for the boar hunt?"

I nod. "The one where his first lieutenant died? Yes, I remember it well. Father was furious. He also feared the wrath of what my grandfather would do to him."

Artan folds his arms over his chest nervously as though uncertain how to tell his side.

I notice the tension in the room thickens. "Sorry. Go on, I'm listening."

He props his elbows onto the table, pressing his hands together, and leans his forehead down touching his fingers, while rubbing the bridge of his nose. as though he's sorting his thoughts. "That was the night I escaped. While the camp was in chaos trying to focus on the lieutenant's injuries, I slipped out of sight. I ran as fast as I could, but as you know, my attempts to flee failed."

I raise a brow. "So, what happened?" I press.

"It wasn't until the next day that your father noticed I was missing, or I assume, because I didn't hear the wolves come for me. By that time, I was a day's journey ahead. I met Bryce along the way."

That perks Thermyah's interest.

Artan continues, "I'd come upon his camp. He'd had a run-in with the same boar that killed the lieutenant, except the beast lost this time. Bryce had the wild hog strung to the fire. When he and his men realized I was alone and harmless, they allowed me shelter for the night. I told them who I was, and we all had a deep discussion about my fate. I patched their tailored clothes and repaired their worn shoes. They decided then that I might be worth keeping."

I don't know whether to believe him. Thinking back to last night has me wondering if Artan and Tharin, teamed up. It's all too convenient. I sit back in my chair and study him. Aside from not having any magic abilities, the one thing I am good at is reading body language.

"I was told I'm the only necromancer that's ever stepped onto the land of Wisteria Keep," Artan says.

"Clearly, not the only necromancer," I counter.

He looks over at Thermyah, as though unsure whether to continue. "Yes, that has crossed my mind as well, considering the vetting the Fae people put outsiders through."

I narrow my stare. "So, how is it that you're just as lucky? And you came back to the House of Zhir, why?"

He smirks. I can tell he doesn't want to answer me. "It was Bryce's idea."

Thermyah's mouth twitches. "Go on."

I don't know why, but I get the feeling Thermyah knows this story and what Artan is telling is for my benefit.

"He's the one who suggested I fake my death—only then would I be truly free," Artan confesses.

"How did you do it?" I ask.

"By making an enchanted cloak. One that could disguise me as a double. I would put the cloak on, and the second *me* would be the one to die."

I gasp. "The cloak you gave me—"

He winks. "It worked out perfectly of course. And I see you made it safely here."

"Yes, but Artan, they will come for me. It's only a matter of time." His confession has me worried.

"Not if they think you're still alive at the House of Zhir. Plus, Sylvie obviously got my message."

"Sylvie? The forest Fae?"

"She's quite the clever Fae, isn't she?"

"Wait a minute." I squint, staring at Artan. "Are you and she—"

"What?" Artan flushes beet red. "Are you kidding? No. Petra, no!" He glances at Thermyah. "Okay, fine. Yes. She and I are a—"

"Shh, don't say it, Artan." I put up my hand. "I don't need the details."

"Do you forgive me?" Artan asks. "I'm sorry for keeping you hanging, but it was the only way to keep you safe."

I nod, giving him a hug. "I forgive you."

"There is one flaw in your brilliant plan, Artan," Thermyah interrupts.

"What's that?"

"Unlike you, where your clone sacrifices their existence so you could escape, Petra's will dissolve once she turns eighteen. They will know the truth at midnight."

"Hang on a minute. I never saw a clone back at the castle."

"No, I suppose you didn't. The moment the Faeries lifted you off the ground and brought you to the blue oak tree, Sylvie cast the cloning spell. I'm betting the soldiers found you in the frozen snow. I mean the other, you."

The back door rattles. We hear keys jingle on the other side, followed by the unlocked latch. "Looks like Bryce is back," Artan says.

Thermyah, of course, bombards him first, saying, "Bryce, you have some explaining to do, young man."

Bryce catches my eye and briskly comes to greet me, ignoring Thermyah's advances. "Hello," he says. "We meet again."

Thermyah's attention is diverted by Artan, and they then begin to argue, getting into a shouting match, about why Artan is here in Wisteria Keep and how he managed to slip through the guarded gates unnoticed.

I suddenly feel flushed. I clear my throat and nod. Half of me loathes Bryce's presence, yet the other half swoons.

Thermyah and Artan stop arguing, and she moves over, saying, "We have important matters to attend to, and we need your assistance, Bryce."

"Very well, Mother. Is Aoes ready?"

"All set," he calls.

Thermyah whispers. "It's time."

21

HALL OF SECRETS

I 'M STILL TRYING TO wrap my head around the fact that this gorgeous man isn't a vampire and happens to be the son of the legendary Eye of the Raven. *Wait, does this mean he has powers, too, like her? The secrets keep piling up. Something has to give soon.*

The three men hurry with unloading the merchandise that arrived from the shipment and then lock the back door.

"Have you seen Kraig?" Thermyah asks Bryce.

"Yes, he asked me to cover his shift and wait for the incoming shipment, which is why I was down by the docks."

"Very well, we can't wait for him. Will you open the Iron Door of Secrets please? Going back to my home is too risky."

Bryce appears taken aback by her request.

"I assure you, son, it is indeed necessary."

He clears his throat. "Right this way." We all follow him to a small walkway that leads to a stairwell behind the counter and cabinets. Once we reach the top step, we enter another dark room. Bryce's eyes begin to glow, sending a ray of blue shades to light up the darkness. An iron door appears in one corner of the room. It's barely visible. I can tell that it's a hidden door and not meant for the average person to see.

"We have about eight hours left to do this ceremonial ritual," Thermyah says. "We can't take any chances of doing this out in the open. At least in here, we're protected from outside forces."

Bryce takes from his pocket a string of keys, picking out one that is of an unusual shape than that of the rest, and places it into the lock. He looks to Thermyah for final approval before turning the key. "Here we go. No backing out once we go in."

"We're prepared," Aoes says.

Passing the threshold, I find nothing fancy about what this door leads to, because all it is, is a tight claustrophobic closet, until someone turns on the light, and I can freely see many boxes and shelves of books. "Not as enchanting as I expected. You've taken me to a closet."

Aoes grunts. "Follow me."

At the end of the room is another door, and I watch in amazement as the frame lights up when Bryce places the same key into another lock. Words appear above the door in a language I cannot understand.

"Hall of Secrets," Aoes says.

The door opens, and beyond the threshold, a cold circular room reveals more doors that line the walls around the space. In the center is a table that can seat fifty people or more. There's a buffet table butted against one wall with a mirror hanging above, and a sooty fireplace is next to it, where Thermyah immediately begins to start a fire.

"Where are we?" I ask.

"A secret portal hub. It's been dormant since the destruction of our sun," Thermyah says.

Artan, appears stunned, too. "I had no idea this survived."

"Only a handful of people know of its existence," Bryce says, gesturing to a chair at the oval table. "Please, have a seat."

We all sit, except Thermyah. She pulls out a standing rack with an attached cauldron tucked next to the hearth. Adjacent to that is a cabinet where she pulls containers of water, which she then pours into the black cast iron pot. "So, tell us more about your dream?" Thermyah asks as she works.

Bryce and Aoes settle across the table, while Artan scoots in beside me.

Looking at each of them, I say, "It was strange. I remember standing in Thermyah's living room when she introduced me to Fate—"

"Wait," Aoes interrupts. "You mean the Fate of Souls?"

"I don't know what he was, but the dark shadowy figure summoned me to his will. I had no control over my body. The next thing I know, I was looking at Thermyah's fate instead of mine." I look over at Thermyah. "Your family's cursed," I blurt. "Am I right?"

Thermyah stops, as though gaining her composure. I've struck a nerve. "Cursed is a strong word, but yes. How do you know?"

"The dream I had last night." I look down at my finger admiring the detail of my new ring. "And this." I hold up my hand. "When I put it on, something called to me."

Thermyah comes to investigate.

Aoes too. "This confirms it, Myah. She has to be the one we've been looking for."

Artan seems confused. "What am I missing?"

Bryce raises a brow shaking his head, at Artan to save the questions for now. "Please continue, Petra."

"It pertained to something about not heeding Meeka's instructions, and Thermyah blames herself for the death of her sister. But what I can't understand is why I was shown Thermyah's past?"

Thermyah gasps dropping her tasks with the fire preparations. Her eyes begin to well with tears. "Sarmira found out about the trade and killed Meeka because of it."

"What trade?" I ask. It finally clicks. "My dream last night wasn't just your past, it was ours, put together. You dreamt the same dream, didn't you?"

She nods. "I found out the day of my sister's death. I'm not proud of my past, but I promised my sister I would make it right, and that's what I'm trying to do now."

"I get it now," Bryce says. He steals a glance at Thermyah. "Why did you keep this secret from us?"

"Because I felt that if you didn't know, the demons of the darkness—Zhir's army, wouldn't reach you."

Bryce stares into space, as though he's recalling a traumatic event. "I was around five. I remember the fires and the burning flesh. I heard a baby screaming." He looks at me.

Thermyah comes to sit with us. "When Meeka and I found you both we had to act quickly. The Zhir army was close and searching for survivors. They wanted no witnesses to the massacre."

Dazed by her confession, my eyes promptly fill with tears. "What?"

She looks at me. "Honestly, I was hoping you would never find out this bit of information. But I know now, that was just wishful thinking." She gazes over at Artan. "But you changed all that."

"So, it's my fault now, is that it?" he answers.

Thermyah laughs. "Faults? I'm not blaming you." She goes back to her work of crushing herbs. "I do have a second chance, though, and I'm not going to waste it."

Aoes adds, "Now we know somewhat of who you are—"

"And who am I, exactly? That hasn't been cleared up."

Aoes smiles as though he understands my curiosity. "As I said before I'm only in my apprentice stage and cannot help beyond my capabilities, but I too had a vision. Though quite different than yours, Petra, I saw the Child of Darkness. Two paths, two different outcomes, but I did not see which choice the child made."

"That's a bit ominous," Artan says. "Who is this Child of Darkness?"

Something doesn't feel right. My ring begins to glow. The rest notice, too. "What's happening?"

A voice calls inside my head, *"The Child of Darkness is your charge. You're to protect her, no matter the cost."*

I gulp. "Did you hear that?"

"Here what?" Bryce asks.

"Only you can hear me."

"Nothing."

"Well, it's something," Aoes says. "You look like you've seen a ghost."

I swallow hard. "You could say that." I look at the ring. "I think it's this."

Aoes takes a closer look. "That's the markings of a Storm ring." He inspects my eyes and then reads my other palm. "My dear, I do believe you're the last in your bloodline." He leans back in his chair studying my face. The palm reading from earlier only gave me your magical abilities, but clearly seeing this ring I have no doubt that you're of Storm blood."

"Aoes, you want to fill us in here?" Bryce asks.

"A Storm?" Artan appears stunned. "But they all—"

"Died?" Aoes finishes. "It appears there was one survivor. Petra wears the Storm ring. Each ring carries a different stone. The eyes of the dragon's head was Lapis Lazuli, representing the Storm Kingdom, and the stone embedded in its jaws is the magical element of their talents. The one Petra wears is all Lapis Lazuli." He pauses, before going further, "Her mother's."

Tears well, as I stare at the three of them, in disbelief. "I can't. I'm a daughter, a princess, from the House of Zhir."

Aoes reaches for my fumbling hands. "You're the Princess of the House of Storm. I bet my life on it."

"How can you be certain?" Artan asks.

"Because only a Storm can wear that ring."

I gasp.

"And the rest of the court wore similar rings," Aoes adds. "What's more important, now that we know, we need to make sure Petra has a proper ceremony."

My mind floods with questions, too many to count. "I want to know more. What do you know of my past?" I ask.

"I don't know much, but what I do know, is your family bloodline fought for what was right and tried to keep the peace, but the Storms were no match for the Zhir army."

"Zhir?" My heart pounds to hear this news. Part of me always wondered. I mean, I look different, act different, and I can't even cast a magic spell. I'm as close as one can be to being human without being human. "Wait, I'm human... that's why I can't cast magic, isn't it?"

Thermyah shakes her head. "No, that's not why. Storms are warrior people. They usually rely on strength, wisdom, and courage. They were a strong species but were no match to the Zhir. They didn't believe in joining their talents with that of other tribes. A proud people that ended up destroying their entire race. The king of your people did not have an open mind and refused to allow for diplomacy. They isolated themselves as a result."

What Thermyah says, isn't true. I can feel deep down that assumption is misunderstood. "My grandfather wouldn't go after a clan for no reason. There had to be something to gain from it."

"You're right," Aoes answers. "It is said at the Circle of Ancestors that there will come a child from the House of Storm that will put an end to the House of Zhir. I'm sure you have many questions," Aoes says, "but that will have to wait until tomorrow."

"And we can't ignore the fact that Sarmira will be searching for her," Bryce says.

Aoes looks over at Artan, answering, "According to him, we have very little time left. The clone of Petra will wear off at midnight."

I smile in spite of the circumstances. Uncle Artan is indeed a clever man. I would have loved to see the look on their faces during the midnight ceremony.

Bryce sighs. "I don't think she will look here in Wisteria Keep. They still think our world is a myth."

"That's where you're wrong," I interrupt. "My mother is convinced this city exists, and if she convinces my grandfather, they will stop at nothing to penetrate these walls."

"Petra, may I see your battle talent for a moment?" Aoes asks.

"You mean that rock?" I huff, still not understanding how that is going to be used to protect me. I pull it out of my Endless Bag.

Setting it on the table it makes a hefty thud, yet when it's in my palm the object feels as though it holds no weight. Aoes goes to grab it but is quickly reminded at how heavy it is for him.

"Wait a second, Aoes," Thermyah says, stopping him. She attempts to pick it up and measures the difficulty it is for her, too. She looks to my uncle. "Artan will you please?" She nods to the large oval rock.

"You mean, pick it up?" he asks.

"Please." She eyes me, briefly, adding, "I have a theory."

He too struggles to handle the stone.

Thermyah chuckles. "Petra, grab the stone, will you?"

Confused by where she's going with this I do as she says. Picking it up with the tips of my fingers effortlessly I hold it up.

Thermyah squints. "That isn't a rock at all, or a geode. Aoes, are you thinking what I'm thinking?"

"That's impossible, that would mean she's—"

"Yep," Thermyah confirms. "We haven't many more hours left in the day."

"That I am what?" I press.

Ignoring my question, Thermyah says, "We're running out of time. Aoes is right, knowing who Petra truly is, if not given a proper ceremony, it will have an impact on her magic after she's eighteen." She stirs the bowl, adding the spices she'd been crushing in the mortar and pestle. Then takes the bracelet Lily made and plops it into the cauldron.

"Wait when did you get the bracelet back from Lily?"

181

Thermyah looks amused. "Annabelle left it on the table over there by the mirror."

"I'm confused."

"Annabelle has access to this portal hub from her shop as well. She has instructions to meet us here soon. In the meantime, she dropped off the bracelet as her and Lily are also preparing for your ceremony."

Thermyah turns to Bryce, handing him a note. "I need you to go to my place and gather these."

He bows his head. "As you wish."

"Make sure you're not followed." She looks to the other men. "And, take these with you." She hands the men vial jars filled with a green liquid, that she grabbed from the cupboard.

"What is this?" Artan asks.

"A protection spell. Drink it now while still shielded behind these walls."

They do as they are instructed.

"What does that do," I ask.

"It tells them if they're in danger. It blocks free will, for a brief time, sending them down a path of absolute perfect timing. They will avoid any dangerous path."

She looks at all three of them. "You only have one hour." She gives two more vials to Bryce. "Give these to Annabelle and Lily, please. Tell her not to take it until she's ready."

He nods, giving her a look of uncertainty.

"She'll understand, Bryce. Trust me," Thermyah says, trying to assure him. "Now, go. We haven't much time."

He nods. "We'll be back as fast as we can, Mother." Together he and the others leave.

22

BETRAYED

TIME IS NO LONGER on our side. It never really was, come to think of it. The words flow in and out as Thermyah gives me the steps to complete the unbinding spell. "Why can't you just use your staff to teleport us to a safe spot?"

Thermyah smiles. "We intend to, but first we need to arm ourselves with potions."

She hands me some scissors. "A lock of your hair please."

"My hair?"

"You seem shocked. Once I complete this spell, these stones will forever be attached to your bloodline."

"What do you mean by attached?"

Thermyah sighs. "Each stone enhances your magical abilities. Now that we know you're a storm, we can proceed forward with that ceremonial ritual."

"I was thinking more along the lines of blood—that's what my mother would have requested for a ritual."

"First, I'm not your mother, and second, anything that deals with blood is dark magic. Remember that.

"I'm placing a protection spell on you so that at the stroke of midnight, your mother will not find you in the future. The bracelet Lily made is in this pot. You must wear it always."

I nod.

"Before we go any further," Thermyah begins, "you must claim the energy as yours." She uncovers the pot of boiling liquid and pulls out the bracelet Lily made. "Each stone represents a magic power. This will give your gifts added protection." She places the bracelet on a towel, allowing it to cool, while explaining each stone and its properties.

"Labradorite is your energy stone. It will heal your mind, body, and soul. It will protect you from dark energies."

She moves to the next stone. "This is Black Tourmaline, as you might already know—"

"Wait a minute..." I check my pocket. They're empty. "How did you—" I gape. "Never mind, I don't want to know."

Thermyah chuckles. "Not to worry, I didn't rummage through your stuff. You gave them to me last night."

"The dream..."

She nods. "As I was saying, the Black Tourmaline will enhance the dark protection. It will allow your thoughts to focus and be clear."

"I notice the center stone is a sapphire," I say, pointing.

"Lapis Lazuli, actually."

I look down at my ring and smile.

"This will give insight and protect you as well."

"And these?" I reference three bright blue stones.

"Aquamarine, blue opal, and turquoise, all will protect you in different ways. Of course, there are three stones of Labradorite, as well. Seventeen stones in all, representing the age you are before your awakening.

She looks over at the geode setting upon the table. At midnight, that will crack open revealing the familiar that is born to you.

"But I thought that is only for Light Witches?" I ask. "I was born on the dark side."

"Have you not figured it out yet?"

I look at her, confused.

"It doesn't matter if you're born to light or dark witches, what matters are the choices you make before your eighteenth birthday. That is what determines you as light or dark." She motions me to put out my wrist. "Besides, the Storm bloodline ancestors all practiced light magic. You make your own decisions, not where you come from, or the bloodline within, but the very will that is given to you. These stones will help guide you to your purpose." She flips the bracelet front to back. "This has cooled. It's time you wear it."

A tingling sensation flows through me as I slip it on.

I feel the bracelet adhere to my skin, searing it. I scream in pain. "It's hurting!" I try to jerk away, but she holds me there.

"The pain will diminish soon." She takes another towel and wraps my wrist in it with ice. "You will be fine."

The pain subsides as quickly as it came. "I don't understand."

"You're forever protected under the Eye of the Raven now."

"What do you mean?" I demand.

"I marked you and your future bloodline for eternity."

"Marked?" The blood beneath my veins boils with rage. "You tricked me."

"More like I didn't tell you everything. I knew if I told you, you wouldn't go through with it."

"Darn right I wouldn't. How could you?" I push away wanting to escape her very presence.

"Listen Petra, you're the last of your bloodline. The prophecy must be fulfilled."

"Prophecy?" I stop.

"I've just guaranteed that it will be accomplished. We will be at war in a few hours' time."

I gasp. "I'm trying to run from chaos, not into it."

"I'm afraid that was never an option. War would still come. We managed to thwart it in a different direction for the time being. If it makes you feel any better. Your running away slowed Vothule down. His intentions were always Wisteria Keep."

"But my grandfather thinks this place is a myth. I told you that."

"I wish that were true."

"Is that why there is this sudden detour in direction. Why we're not going to the gates of Ladorielle?"

"If Annabelle and I hadn't seen your grandfather's plans, it would have left us vulnerable. At least we have a fighting chance when they arrive."

"Arrive?"

"They're marching here now."

"How do you know?"

"I'm a seer, remember?"

"But you said it was subjective."

"It is. Not to worry, though, you're in good hands. I've made sure that your destiny is fulfilled."

Fear consumes me, along with anger. I haven't the words to speak. I feel utterly betrayed.

"You may begin to feel different." I watch Thermyah pour more liquid into a mug. "Now, drink this, it will help with the pain."

"I'm supposed to trust you now, after what you just pulled?" I feel trapped, just like I did living under the House of Zhir. I was never really free. Not in the Eye of the Raven's eyes. She knew who I was from the very beginning. They all played along. And the rest of them—Aoes, Bryce, and Artan, do they know her like I do?

"Let me help you understand. Sarmira wants your grandfather's throne." Thermyah huffs.

"I already suspected that. It's why I stole the plans from my grandfather's study." Suddenly, it hits me. My thoughts immediately go to the book I found hidden in Grandfather's desk. "The plans." I look at Thermyah. "I left the plans hidden inside the *Book of Secrets*. My grandfather was planning this attack way before I spontaneously ran away."

Thermyah nods. "Yes, and you let me see them, remember?"

A sharp pain enters my side, and I double over in agony. I feel burning heat flow through me, and my head begins to build pressure with excruciating throbs. The pulsation is so intense that it sends me to my knees. I lie down feeling incredibly weak.

I gasp. "What have you done to me?" I tuck my chin to my chest and curl into a fetal position, hugging my pounding head.

"Drink the tea, it's the only thing that can save you now."

I clinch my teeth holding onto every word, saying, "I'm supposed to believe you?"

"If you don't drink it, you'll die."

"You cursed me like my mother did to your sister. Is this your way of getting back at Sarmira?"

Thermyah bends down, handing me the magical cure. "No, not at all. It's called leverage, my dear." She smiles. "Your choice. What will it be? Live, or die?" She sets the cup next to my head, on the floor.

I listen to her stinging words. I don't know whether to thank her or hate her right now. I feel tricked. I'm caught in a conundrum. It doesn't matter which way I choose. I won't be free. Magic has a price. I've always known that but at what cost will I have to pay it? I have no choice. I drink the tea.

23

IT'S TIME

I WANTED FREEDOM. I wanted to travel to Ladorielle. Why couldn't she grant me that? Now I and my line is forever marked. I glare at Thermyah with venom. I drink the tea, and just as she mentioned, it cures the pain, but it costs me more than I bargained for.

"I don't expect you to understand," she says.

"You're right, I don't." I sneer. "Forcing me to become like you! That was your game this entire time."

"You wanted freedom. I gave you that."

I watch as she takes the remaining cooled liquid from her cauldron and pours it into small vial jars. "If you wanted to sever ties with your past and look to the future, the unbinding spell I perform had to be done." She gives a satisfied grin. "You will understand later."

I resent her remark. It's too late now. I'm going to have to live with my mistake for the rest of my life. "Is this when you tell me to be careful what you wish for?"

Thermyah grunts. "Ah, yes, I suppose it does seem like that. I'm not asking for your approval. What's done is done. We're moving on with the ritual, and you still must choose a side."

"What if I don't choose? What if I renounce my rites of passage?"

"If only it were that simple. You always have a choice. You can either continue down the path of avoiding your calling and hide from your mother or become more powerful than her. Either way, you must choose. And not choosing is still yet a choice."

"I didn't have much of a choice when you cursed me just now," I spat. "I'll never forgive you for what you've done." I glare at her, and my soul fills with hatred. "And now you give me some sort of riddle about choices?"

"Take it how you see fit. But come midnight by not choosing, the choice will be made for you. Time does not wait for anyone. You will still turn eighteen. And as I mentioned before, not making a choice will send you to Scarlet Hollow."

Scarlet Hollow. I'd forgotten about that.

"The very second the clock strikes midnight you will begin feeling the magic inside you stir. There will be both good and bad. The war within your mind will begin to awake."

Thermyah takes a long pause and then looks at me. "There's a fifth to the elements you know."

"A fifth?"

Thermyah makes a fist and then puts out her palm toward me, turning her wrist upward. She uncurls her fingers, revealing a butterfly sitting on her hand. "Magic."

"H-how did you do that?"

"You know, there is magic in every being that exists. It's how one taps into it that changes. Like this butterfly."

I watch as the creature flutters around.

"Life as we know it goes through a metamorphosis. We grow inside our own world, learning and seeking growth. When we reach our desired limits of what we feel has been completed, the transformation begins." She looks deep into my eyes. "You will be eighteen in a matter of minutes. It's time to choose. Light or dark?"

"Seems I'm choosing dark or grey. What part of light magic is there when you just forced me to be your protégé?"

She stops looking at the butterfly as it lands on the framed mirror. "Your transformation will be your identity."

An alarm sounds, startling us.

"Grab your geode, Petra," Thermyah says.

I do as she says, asking, "What's going on?"

Before Thermyah answers, the door to the shop opens, and in comes Kraig, Artan, and Bryce, followed by two other familiar faces, Annabelle and Lily.

"Petra," Lily says, and runs to my side. "They're coming for us. They have found a way into Wisteria Keep."

I don't like the sound of fear in Lily's voice. Which can only mean one thing. "My mother." The anger returns and to at Thermyah. "You said Wisteria Keep was safe."

"I also said war was inevitable." She looks up at Bryce. "How bad is it?"

"They've breached the invisible bridge."

I hear Thermyah swear under her breath. "We've wasted so much time."

"I have an idea," Aoes suggests. "Where's the book?"

"I have it right here," Thermyah says as she pulls it from her Endless Bag. She hands the book over to Aoes. "Although I wouldn't open it."

He inspects the outside of the book. "Where are the plans?" He looks up at me.

"Behind the front cover," I say. I look at the clock. "Five minutes to go."

The hub shakes, and we all brace ourselves.

"We better hurry," Annabelle says. "They're going to find us."

The look of astonishment, on Aoes's face shocks me. "You opened the book and didn't leap to another place and time?"

I nod my head. "Of course not." I look at Kraig, remembering he was just as shocked when I opened it earlier this morning.

"You're not Fae," Aoes says. "How did you—"

Another blast, shakes the portal hub.

"The only way to open this book is either by a Fae, or the book itself," he says.

I tilt my head. "Come again?" I realize then that there is no doubt, Tharin knew exactly what that book was. I only wish he lived long enough for me to confront him.

"Dust," Aoes says. "Fae dust prevents the book from banishing you. Another possible way is the magic of the book itself. It will choose a destination, for you." He glances over at the empty pedestal that sets upon a circular pentagram, that is embedded into the marble stone floor. "Unless..."

Aoes places the book on the podium.

The book immediately lights up, the cover opens on its own, and the pages begin to violently flip, sending swirling gusts into the circular room.

Thermyah looks at the clock. "Three minutes to go. It's going to be close."

The forceful magical winds pull me close to the book, and I try with all my strength to hold my ground. "Thermyah, what aren't you telling us?" I ask. "This doesn't feel right."

"A portal is about to open," Thermyah warns. "The balance of the realms are offset. Brace yourself, everyone."

She hands me the stone she gave me as a little girl. "There is no time for me to explain. You must hold onto this and no matter how much you want to drop it you mustn't let go. Your life depends upon it."

I seethe. "Yeah, where have I heard that before?"

Thermyah glares at me as though in some unspoken words, she's telling me the truth. I can see it in her eyes.

The wind ceases, and the pages stop flipping, landing on their destination. A doorframe behind us lights up.

Avoiding the distraction, I ask, "How did you get ahold of this?" Seeing the Hawke's Eye in my hand, I check my pockets and realize they're empty.

"No time to explain," she says.

A searing burning sensation penetrates my palm and I scream in agony once again. My tender flesh bakes beneath the stone. "I can't handle it." I try to drop it, but Thermyah holds my hand shut, looking at me with tears in her eyes. "I'm sorry, my child, I hope you can one day forgive me."

"We can't hold them off," I hear Artan yell, as he braces against the door that leads to the shop.

"Thirty seconds," Thermyah says. "Steady yourselves. We're cutting this real close."

"For what?" I ask.

"Impact." She eyes the clock intently. "Ten seconds until midnight."

"Thermyah, what do we do?" Annabelle asks.

Nine.

"Keep Petra in the hub as long as we can until the last second. Stand near the podium and wait for that gate to open."

Eight.

A blast is heard outside the shop door, forcing Artan to fall.

Seven.

"Artan, run now!" Bryce calls.

"Are we going to die?" I ask.

I watch the clock's second hand.

Six.

Five.

The portal gate opens behind us. I hear someone say, "Jump now."

Annabelle, and Lily disappear through the portal, first.

Four.

"Go now," Aoes says. "I'll hold them back."

Three.

"No, you can't, you'll die," Thermyah protests.

Aoes pushes her through the gate.

Two.

"I'm staying, too," Artan says.

"No!" I scream. I feel a hand grab my arm, pulling me through the portal.

One.

The portal gate shuts, and I emerge into darkness.

24

A NEW WORLD

M Y LANDING IS HARD. I half expected to incinerate
into nothingness, passing through the portal gate
but instead, I find myself surrounded by trees. Rather than
it be midnight, of my birthday, it's midafternoon. I stand to
gather my composure but immediately sit back down, feeling
a bit queasy. I look around and don't see anyone I know. I'm
alone.

I look up and see white clouds shade a blue sky. Unfamiliar
sounds of birds singing, and a cold breeze feels soft against my
skin. A chill runs up my spine. I look up to see the sun, but
no moons. Definitely not on Elleirodal.

The trees are slightly different than in my kingdom, too.
Much greener, and the fragrant smells of flowers perk my
senses.

Water trickles nearby, prompting me to follow the sound, when I hear a moan not too far away. The low rumble clues me in that it's a man.

Deep in my soul I pray it is Bryce. Artan and Aoes stayed behind. My heart sinks as I gather the memories. Wisteria Keep is gone, and it's all my fault.

Following the sounds of the moans, I observe that the forest I'm in looks strange with gravel walkways, and trimmed bushes. Flowers are strategically placed in a nearby garden and line the pathway. The sound of the moans and the water seems to blend together the closer I approach. Veering off the trail, I trip and fall. Looking down I realize it's a person's foot.

"Ow," he shouts.

"Bryce!"

He rolls over. "My head." Squinting, he looks at me. "Petra?"

"Yes, it's me." I see a nasty bump on his head. "You're hurt." Blood drips down the side of his temple. I grab a cloth from my pack. "Here, this might help."

"Any sign of the others?" He takes the cloth, wiping the blood.

"No, just you. Where do you suppose we are?"

Bryce looks over his shoulder. "No clue."

"Can you stand?" I ask.

"I think so."

I help him up, and that's when we both notice were not in the woods but a large park.

"Guess that explains the landscaping," I say.

"Yes, but where are we?" Bryce asks, turning a full circle. "I mean this place looks strange."

I follow Bryce's gaze and we spot a man sitting on a park bench reading a large book. It's a strange-looking book, too, it hasn't any cover. But the amazing part, birds flock at his feet eating breadcrumbs.

I step forward, inching my way to the stranger, saying, "Pardon me."

The elderly man looks up. Wire-looking spectacles bridge his nose. He acts surprised, flinching backward. "I haven't any money." He looks us up and down, putting his hands up.

"We don't want your money," Bryce says.

The man relaxes, saying, "Oh?" He folds the large book in half. "Then what, my newspaper? Here take it. I was done reading, anyway." He sets it down beside the bench. Piercing a suspicious glance, he adds, "You know, Halloween isn't for another seven months."

"Halloween?" I ask, puzzled.

The man throws his hands up. "Oh, you kids these days." He gets up from his seat and wanders off slowly, taking with him a strange-looking stick to help him walk.

Bryce picks up the large book, that the man called a newspaper. "It's written in the same language as ours, back home."

"Well, that's a relief," I say, "at least we can read these words."

"Something really weird is going on."

We can't see anything but trees, but we can hear people and strange sounds like horns blowing and loud rumbles.

"Look at this," Bryce says. "The front of the paper March 20th, 1999."

Stunned, by what I see, I say, "What?"

"Maybe we should try and find Annabelle, Lily, and Thermyah."

We walk farther down the path until we reach the end, stepping into a crowded city. There are people everywhere, and strange-looking streets that are not made of cobblestone, but a dark grey surface. And the buildings are so tall that I wonder how anyone could climb so many stairs to get to the top.

An unusual contraption, much like the one that nearly ran me over the other day, speeds by.

"We're definitely not on Elleirodal anymore," Bryce says.

I reach into my back pocket and discover a piece of paper tucked inside. Wrinkling my forehead, I pull it out.

"What is that?" Bryce asks.

I shrug and unfold it.

Dearest Petra,

There is so much I wish I could say to you, but alas we ran out of time.

We had to protect you, no matter the cost. You're the last in your bloodline. You must find the other tomes. It's the only way to restore our order. Remember magic comes with a price, so choose wisely. The Hawke's Eye will guide you to the other twelve books. The power of our world will grow, with each book that is restored.

Do not look for us, or Sarmira will find you. Check your Endless Bag. I've left both you and Bryce a gift.

Thermyah

I look at my hand seeing the Hawke's Eye tattooed to my palm. "What does this mean?" My heart pounds. "We're in a strange new world. How are we to get back?"

Bryce takes my hand, saying, "I don't know, but we will do it together."

COMPLETED BOOK LIST

I hope you enjoyed reading Eye of the Raven.
If possible I would appreciate an honest review.
Reviews help so much! Thank you!
Here is the complete book list.

Storm Bloodline Saga

Prequel: Eye of the Raven

Book 1: Eyes of Wynter

Book 2: Different Shade of Wynter

Book 3: Wynter Reign

Book 4: Wynter's Fury

House Trilogies

Part of the Storm Bloodline Saga

Vol 1: House of Shadow Raven

Mirror of Fate

(Coming soon)

Mirror of Souls

Mirror of Darkness

Other Books

The Fairy Mermaid and the Crystal Key

JOIN EMMY'S NEWSLETTER

Want to be notified the minute Emmy releases her next book? Sign up for her newsletter to get sneak peeks of cover reveals, exclusive content and new release announcements or go to Emmy's Website: erbennettbooks.com

Come follow Emmy on:

TicTok

Twitter

Emmy's Creative Corner

Instagram

<u>Bookbub</u>

Facebook

Join Emmy's mailing list

ABOUT THE AUTHOR

©Photography by Mel Sabarez

Emmy R. Bennett lives in Pacific Northwest with her husband, two children, and their two dogs. She also has two adult children.

When she isn't at her desk writing, she's spending time with her family, gardening, crafting, or reading.

Emmy grew up in a Lutheran household. Although she's strong in her faith, she believes everyone has the right of free will in their beliefs.

She loves to study genealogy, and her family line has been traced back to the Vikings. It's one of the many inspirations from which she's drawn to write.